The Kid in th

By

Noah Baldonado

And

Richard Williams

Baldonado Brothers Books

The Kid in the Lamborghini

Chapter 1

Noah sat in his dad's pickup truck. It was an almost new black 2018 Ford F-150 in mint condition, and his dad had brought it home the night before. Things had been pretty tough around the house lately, and Noah thought he actually saw him smile a little.

It was a cloudy late afternoon in the Gilbert, Arizona fall. Labor Day had come and gone, and now each day seemed the same. Get up, get breakfast, get to school, get bored in seventh grade, get home and then get a lecture from his dad about how important it was not to get bored in school. Summer vacation was long over, and Halloween seemed forever away.

When people looked at Noah, they might assume he was a typical 12-year-old seventh grade boy. He was 5'5" and weighed 125 pounds. He had a pile of curly brown hair on his head, which invited guesses as to which way it was going, and deep brown eyes that were always curious and observant.

His dad knew he loved anything with an engine. Accordingly, he had promptly instructed him to never get into the new truck alone. It was beautiful and looked even better than the advertisements.

After dinner, his dad said he was going to shower. He took long showers, so Noah took the keys from the table, clicked the open button, went outside and climbed in. He figured he could be out and have the keys back before his dad finished. As was his way, he knew everything about the truck before his dad brought it home. It had the new ten speed transmission, a reverse backup camera, and an online connection system.

He paused and took a picture of his Mom out from his pocket and looked at it. He missed her but usually wouldn't let himself look at her picture. It made him too sad. He put it back in his shirt pocket and looked around the truck cab. It smelled clean and new, and all the instruments and controls made him feel like he was in a jet cockpit—his dream job.

He reached forward and started to take the gearshift in his hand. Before he could touch the knob, however, he froze. Without any ignition or activation of the truck, the instrument panel had suddenly lit up. In the middle of the navigation screen, he saw the brightly displayed words "Hello Noah." Startled, he leaned in to look at the screen and controls more closely. He was close to the screen, and a moment later, heard a voice speak very clearly.

"Hello, Noah."

He jerked back and away from the screen in shock, and accidentally hit the parking brake pedal with an extended foot. The screen went dark, and then everything fell apart. Even though the gearshift was set to park, the truck started to roll backwards. He felt it moving down the slight hill of their driveway. He checked the gears again and tried to move the gearshift. It wouldn't budge. He pushed the brake pedal but got no response. The truck kept moving and picked up speed. He reacted quickly, and pushed the emergency brake back into position, but not before the rear bumper struck the mailbox post. The mailbox and post snapped cleanly away from the cement base and hit the street with a large metallic *bang!*

He jumped from the truck and looked at the back bumper. There were several scrapes and a large dent on the left side. The front door of the house opened, and his dad in his bathrobe strode angrily across the lawn towards the truck. He held out his hand to Noah for the key. Noah put the key in his hand and started to speak.

Dad cut him off. "Up to bed. Now."

Noah paused for a second and tried to think of how he could explain what happened. "The truck talked to me."

His father shook his head and became even more angry. "Now."

Noah walked slowly up the stairs and trudged into his room. He knew that bed meant lights out. No reading, web searches for pictures of cars, or videos of performance cars. It was a terrible, boring end to a boring, lonesome day in a house that always seemed so empty. He crawled in bed and felt himself choke up a little, although he couldn't say why.

Chapter 2

Noah was troubled when he woke up the next morning, and immediately after opening his eyes remembered why. He walked to the window. The broken mailbox lay in the street, and he realized it had not been just a bad dream. His shoulders sagged as he trudged over to his chest of drawers and put on the first shirt and pair of shorts in reach. He stood for a moment and heard the television downstairs. He dreaded seeing his dad. As he walked down the stairs, one memory of the pickup truck continued to bother him. The truck had said his name. Why? How?

He entered the kitchen and saw his dad sitting at the table, watching the flat screen TV on the wall. On the table Noah saw a large chocolate sprinkled donut sitting next to a bowl of Special K. This was his favorite breakfast, and his dad had set it up for him. It had been hard for both of them since losing his mother. For a long time he would often hear his dad cry through the closed bedroom door when he thought Noah was sleeping. The new truck had been one of the few things that made his dad happy.

His dad turned to him from the TV. "Good morning, buddy."

Noah sat down, still upset that he had angered his father. "Good morning." He was quiet and began to eat.

His dad spoke again. "Don't worry about the truck. It's just a machine. It's just metal and plastic, and you didn't really hurt anything. I'm sorry I was so upset."

Noah looked at his dad. "I know you love that truck. I didn't mean for it to roll, but I could have sworn it said my name. With the ignition off. It made me jump."

His dad shrugged and smiled. "I think you probably hear every car call your name. No big deal. I'll replant the mailbox this morning and get the truck bumper fixed. All will be well." He turned to the TV and gestured at it.

"Have you seen this?" On the screen was a video of a helicopter crash. His dad continued. "That's the second copter crash in 3 days. Both were military, and both crashes were just out of Albuquerque. There was also a huge freeway pileup this morning on the I-40 just east out of town, and two more on the I-25."

Albuquerque was special since it was where his dad's parents lived. They loved Noah, and his earliest memories of their home always made him smile. Every trip to their home on San Luis Place just off the I-40 made him feel like he was the most important boy in the world. Grandpa Tony taught him about cars and baseball, and Grandma Liz made tacos that he couldn't stop eating, while teaching him bits and pieces of Spanish. He was their *hijito*, and they treated him like a prince. He loved to go in his dad's old room at the house and stare at his sports trophies. He also enjoyed the old pictures of his dad—the two of them looked almost exactly alike.

He leaned toward the television. The voice over was saying that there were major traffic accidents on every freeway heading out of Albuquerque. Nothing like this had ever happened before, and traffic was paralyzed. His dad shook his head.

"I've never seen anything like it. The freeways are shut down, and a plane just skidded off the runway and crashed at the Sunport. Now the airport is closed. Wow. There's no way to get in or out of town."

Dad looked at the clock and turned off the television. He got up and grabbed his jacket. "Do you want me to drop you off at school?"

Noah shook his head. "No thanks. I'm plenty early and feel like walking. I may meet up with some of my friends on the way."

He grabbed his backpack and walked out the door. They hugged, and as he walked down the sidewalk toward school, his dad got in the truck, backed out, and slowed down near Noah on the sidewalk. He rolled down the window.

"If the truck asks for you, should I call you or just take a message?

Noah tried not to smile. "Too soon, Dad." But he couldn't stop the grin. His dad grinned back and drove away.

He went another block. The school was a mile from his house, and he decided to try a short cut down a side street. The street bordered a park, and opposite the park were two empty lots. He was deep in thought when he reached the middle of the block. To his right, he heard a car start in the asphalt lot of the park. Not just any car, however. Over the years, he had watched hundreds of videos of cars, and the engine he heard was not a regular car. The sound was a deep rumble mixed with a roar, and it sounded like money. Lots of money.

He spun around to the engine sound. His mouth opened in amazement when he saw a dark grey, sleek machine which looked more like a fighter jet than a car starting to pull out of the lot. He knew instantly what it was—a Lamborghini Veneno Roadster, the 740 horsepower V12 legendary masterpiece. These were the elite cars of all elite cars. There were only nine produced, and they each sold at over 4.5 million dollars. They were designed to move faster than anything else on the ground. He stared in disbelief as the car moved slowly toward the street. A Veneno in the little park on his way to school in Gilbert, Arizona? He shook his head and then stood gaping. It looked like a low-flying spaceship coming toward him. He would have been less surprised to have found the actual *Mona Lisa* sticking out of a garbage can near the park.

The windows were darkly tinted. He strained to see a driver, but could see no one. He stood motionless, expecting to see the car shoot away down the street, but instead it pulled slowly to a stop in front of him. The engine stopped. The car seemed to wait expectantly. Suddenly, the driver's side door opened smoothly, lifting up like a wing in the famous "scissor" style. He waited. Nobody got out, and not a sound came from the dark car.

He stood a full minute. There was no traffic, and the park was quiet. He couldn't stop himself from slowly walking around the back of the car to the driver's side. He peered at the elaborate cockpit of carbon fiber and past the leather steering wheel to the instrument panel. The Lamborghini lion was in majestic profile on the wheel.

He was shocked to find that the car was empty. Nobody in the front seat, nobody in the back seat, and no signs that anyone had been there. He was careful not to touch the car, and it took every bit of his willpower to resist climbing into the driver's seat. However, having learned his lesson from the yesterday's disaster with the pickup, he reluctantly turned and started to walk away. His heart sunk as the distance grew between him and the car. He was certain that this would be the first and last time he would ever see such a car. Most of his friends would have no idea what a Veneno roadster was, and those that did would never believe he saw one on the way to school moving down the street with no driver.

He was no more than 20 feet away when he heard the car start again. He stopped again and turned back. The door was still open. He had the strange feeling that the car was calling to him. He slowly approached the car yet again and then, reaching the door again, stopped when he heard a voice. It was the same voice, the exact same voice as yesterday. He listened in disbelief as the voice calmly repeated what it said before he had panicked and the truck had rolled down the driveway.

"Hello, Noah."

Chapter 3

Noah leaned into the car and looked carefully around the interior. This time he noticed a small black box, about the size of a shoebox, sitting on the back seat. It was held securely by two leather straps coming from the seat itself. He felt the straps. They were firm but stretched with a little effort. He reached toward the box, and a voice again surrounded him from the speakers of the car.

"Careful. Don't rub my casing. If you create a static field around me, it might interfere with my neural network and increase the chances of inaccurate data reception and transmission." He pulled his hand away from the box.

"Thank you. Would you like to get in?"

He backed away slightly. "No." He added, "No, thank you," although he wasn't sure to whom he was being polite.

The car, or the box inside the car, spoke again. "That's very wise. No young person should ever get in an unfamiliar car. However, if you hear me out, I think I will be able to show you that I am quite familiar with you, and soon you will be familiar with me."

He was silent, processing, wondering, and thinking a thousand things at once. He spoke up again.

"Who are you? Are you the box? Are you part of the car?"

The voice came back. "I am not part of the car, although I control it. My hardware is in the black box. It is 8 by 12 inches in dimension, weighs 3 pounds, and is entirely highly conductive silicon and plastic. I am an intelligence entity created by the United States Department of Defense. I control this car and its features in order to assist you. There is a 25-year lithium power source and the most sensitive signal receptors in the universe within my casing. I am in contact with the largest computer system in the world, which is part of the Department of Defense of the United States of America. This box allows me to communicate with you by controlling the car, but I am also able to access any information of any type on any system."

Noah took it all in. He was surprised to realize he wasn't afraid but comfortable conversing with whatever this thing was. "Assist me with what?"

"I'm afraid we'll need to discuss that after we get underway. We have a very tight schedule ahead of us. We have only four days to complete a highly secret and somewhat hazardous mission."

"I'm not going anywhere until I know more about you and whatever this schedule is for."

He thought he heard a sigh, although it might have been the morning breeze blowing gently around the open door.

"Why don't I start by explaining a few things regarding you? Your name is Noah Richard Baldonado. You were born June 6, 2008. You are in seventh grade at Greenfield Junior High School in Gilbert, Arizona. School has been in session for approximately seven weeks, and your father is not aware that you have not yet turned in any assignments or scored a passing grade on any tests. You read car magazines in class, which you pay for by skipping lunch and using the money you saved. You pay no attention to the instructors. You are failing all classes. You and your father live at 2845 West Aviary Way, and your mother—"

Embarrassed, Noah protested weakly. "I'm not failing *all* of my classes. I have a D in math."

"You are actually now failing math. You scored 53% correct on the quiz on fractional division yesterday. Your grade dropped from 61 to 58 points out of 100. You are officially now an F student in that class, as well as the others."

The voice kept going, but he'd heard enough. He interrupted. "Okay, okay. What about you?"

"I have told you everything relevant to me. This specific version of me was brought online two weeks ago. Since that time, I have been continuously running simulations and models predictive of our possible encounters and journey. I am running them now, as we are speaking. I am planning a route to the Pentagon at 1400 Defense, Washington, DC. It is a 2,296 mile journey by the safest route."

Intrigued, Noah decided to play along with whatever was going on.

"Suppose I decide to come along—even though there's no way I will. I'm supposed to be in school in 20 minutes. If I'm not there, then call my dad."

"You are no longer expected at school. A phone call from a voice identifying itself as your father was received by the school 5 minutes ago. The voice was a perfect sonic match and used his previously established password for verification. The school was informed that you will be gone for five days, visiting your Aunt Julie in Albuquerque, New Mexico. She is fine, but for the purposes of the phone call, physician and hospital records will show she is ill but will survive."

He had been skeptical, but now had to admit to himself that something very real but very strange was happening.

"What will my dad do when I don't come home for five days?"

"In one hour, your father will receive a phone call via cellular connection. The calling number will be shown as being from Greenfield Junior High School. It will be a

17

speakerphone call using your voice and the voice of Mr. Williams, your science teacher. Your father will be informed that you forgot to provide him with information and permission slips to a 5-day science trip to the Sandia Nuclear Research Laboratory in Albuquerque, New Mexico. He will be informed by both of you that attendance is essential for passing the course. He will receive an email with a permission slip, and another email for return. He will be told you are being issued basic clothing and personal items. He will agree, since he suspects your school performance is very poor. He will not enjoy his time alone while you are gone."

Noah began to have the strangest feeling. It was as if his life prior to this moment had been an intensely boring dream, full of sadness and monotony. He was startled at feeling so awake, so alive. Suddenly, the trees were deeper green. The flowers by the park smelled sweet. The background noise sharpened into distinct sounds, and he was aware of each sound's location and meaning.

He paused for another moment, and after shaking off the slightest hesitation, stepped into the front seat. He closed the door. The unmistakable rumble of the engine immediately hushed to almost nothing. The climate control was set perfectly, as was the seat height. He buckled his shoulder strap and noticed the mirrors were set perfectly, as if he had owned it for years.

Everything about the car seemed familiar, and the idea of driving it seemed no more complicated than riding his bike. The Lamborghini started slowly down the street. A route map appeared on the dash in front of him. The car was driving itself. As if it could sense what he was thinking, the voice spoke.

"You'll be driving soon, but first let me get us on the road. We're short on time."

"Where are we going?"

"We are going to pick up an object from the Sandia National Laboratory of Nuclear Energy in Albuquerque, New Mexico."

"I'm a 12 year old kid driving the most expensive vehicle every made. How will we make it without getting stopped? The minute a state trooper spots us, this ride is over."

"Not necessarily," replied the intelligence unit. "This vehicle is equipped with the most sophisticated day or night external holographic projection system ever deployed. Look at the console and I will show you what anyone outside of the vehicle sees when they look at us. You will be viewing a magnified satellite feed of our journey. You may access it anytime by pressing the SAT button on the center console."

He looked at the screen on the center console in surprise. The video did not show a Lamborghini Veneno with a rather intimidated young boy at the wheel. It showed a dumpy, rusted 1998 Pontiac Minivan, driving the exact same route. The left front wheel was a temporary spare, and the left rear side window had been replaced by cardboard and duct tape. At the wheel, still looking a bit bewildered, was an aging hippie complete with a greying ponytail and tie-dyed t-shirt. The car was a crazy pattern of paints, with giant scrolls of bright colors clashing from front to back.

"We look terrible," he protested. "Why do we have to look so bad?"

"We'll be changing appearance frequently. There are extremely dangerous people looking for us who will destroy us both if we're caught."

"That's great," Noah said sarcastically. "I guess you can fill me in on the details when they start chasing us. It must be my good luck."

The car continued to rumble smoothly down the frontage road, heading for the 60 East. The machine replied patiently. "Luck had absolutely nothing to do with your selection. When I did a national simulation combining the least expected route to the Sandia National Laboratory, the person with the greatest knowledge of this automobile, as well as the person least likely to refuse the mission, you were the first choice by an order of magnitude."

While he wanted to argue, Noah had to admit that he was excited in spite of any danger. He was already beginning to love the feeling of uncertainty and adventure.

"What else can this thing do?" he inquired. "Can it fly?"

"There is a great deal of functionality in this vehicle, but it cannot fly. You will learn most it as we travel, but it may be useful to understand a little at this time."

The glove compartment door opened. Instead of space, there was a small touch screen over an ATM-style slot, with a complicated menu. Noah leaned over and looked at the machine and touched the screen. It scrolled to reveal pictures of different currencies, different credit cards, and different forms of identification.

"So, we have a printer that forges money, credit cards, and ID?"

"You are correct that this machine will produce many personal and financial items, such as money, credit cards, and identification items such as a passport. However, you are incorrect in concluding that the items produced are forgeries. It will actively produce valid, genuine currency for over 100 countries. It will produce credit cards which have no credit limit, are untraceable, and are completely legal. All passports and identification documents are automatically registered with the related government agencies and will not be questioned in any way."

"You're telling me that I could print any of these things I want? I could print a million dollars or take an unlimited credit card?"

"Yes," responded the machine, sounding to Noah as if it were tired of explaining. "But you won't."

"How do you know?"

"Because I know everything about you. I know how much you weighed when you were born. I know the first word you said—your Mother posted the video online. I have reviewed every email you've ever written, every website you've ever been to, every evaluation by any teacher you've ever had, everything you've ever bought. You simply would not do anything dishonest or take anything which does not belong to you."

Noah had a funny feeling—like someone had been looking in his window, watching him, and he knew nothing about it. But the voice was right. He wouldn't dream of taking money or credit cards. It just wouldn't feel.....*right*. He leaned back slightly in the seat.

"Okay," he said. "let's go to Albuquerque. Can you teach me to drive this thing?"

Her voice came back to him, sounding more familiar.

"You already know how to drive this thing. I'll watch you, though. There's a button on the dash which switches off the self-driving feature. Turn it off, and you're in control."

He pushed the button, switched off the self-drive, and took over. The car seemed to glide past the fields and occasional house into the late afternoon sun as if it were the most natural thing in the world. He merged the car onto the 60 East freeway, and as he did, a carful of kids in the next lane riding in a Chrysler Pacifica laughed and waved at the ponytailed old hippie.

4 Chapter

Driving had always looked easy. Maybe it was the car, and maybe it was just that he still couldn't believe that he was behind the wheel of a Lamborghini Veneno—the world's greatest car—but now it all seemed so easy. He had probably watched hundreds of videos of the car racing, touring exotic world highways, and sitting in the garages of billionaires, yet here he was heading southeast out of his hometown in a Veneno. Even for these cars, it had amazing features, and apparently its own brain. The car was comfortable. Someone, or something, had made it fit his 5'5" frame perfectly.

Admittedly, some of the features of this car made it a little easier to drive. Specifically, when he would change lanes, turn, or move, the voice in the car would advise him as to when it was safe. He still felt weird hearing the car speak to him. The voice sounded like a woman in her thirties— smooth, self-assured, with perfect diction and none of the hesitation or monotone of the computerized synthetic voices he'd heard in the past.

He had been driving quietly for some time. The traffic was thin, and the signs said that he was now on the portion of the 60 called the Superstition Highway. As the driving became easier with time, he started to ask questions. The first one seemed obvious.

"Can you play music while I'm driving?"

There were a few moments of silence. Then the machine answered. "It is possible that I can access music files and play them while you are driving. However, you are being constantly monitored during this drive, and I must be careful not to use files or volumes in playback in ways that may distract you."

He shrugged. A black corvette pulled in front of him. *Peasants*, he thought, and smiled.

"Next question." He waited a minute, not taking his eyes off the road. "What is your name?"

Again, there was a pause, but not as long as the one before. "By name, I assume you are wondering how to address me. As a connected device, I am constantly being contacted and referred to by my internet protocol address, which is 0606:2008:1208:2005:0928:1981:0128:1983. You may feel free to address me the same way."

Noah laughed. "I don't think so. You need a name— something simple that I can remember."

"Why?" said the voice. "I don't have a need to establish an identity. I am an AI construct, with no personality or gender."

"Well," said Noah. "I might be more comfortable with the whole setup if I don't have to call you a chain of numbers." He paused for a second. "Let's see. You said you were an AI construct. AI is pronounced *aye*, so maybe you can take a name with that sound." He thought for another second. "Okay. I say we use Eileen. That's a little old fashioned but manages to cover all the bases. It has AI in it, and it's a lady's name—which fits your voice."

The machine replied. "My voice is designed to be maximally calming and reassuring in any situation. "

"Fine," said Noah. "Now can you please tell me where we are going?"

"We are initially proceeding southeast, taking US Highway 60 as we prepare to cross into New Mexico," said Eileen. "We will travel through several small cities and towns, including Globe, Arizona. I thought that might make you happy.

Noah was puzzled. "Why would it?"

The machine seemed to hesitate. "I know people can be very sentimental regarding their family, even if they are no longer living. We will be passing by the burial site of one of your family."

Noah was intrigued. "What are you talking about?"

There was quiet for a moment. Then, Eileen asked a question in response. "You are not aware of any of the burial sites of your ancestors?"

Noah answered a little defensively. "I know where some of my ancestors are buried. My great-grandparents are buried in the Mesa City Cemetery. Another great-grandparent is buried in California. But I don't know who you are talking about."

There was a slight pause as they continued driving down the freeway. Then Eileen said: "Your grandfather's grandfather's grandfather was a cattle rancher in Globe, Arizona. He was born in 1850 and died in 1932. He is buried in the Pinal Cemetery in that city. That is an old cemetery currently under the care of the US Forest Service."

Noah was curious. "What else do you know about him?"

"He was called E.B. by his family. His last name was Wever. He was an interesting man. His father was hung from the neck and killed by a group of men called a posse after he supplied a horse to a young man who was being hunted. His brother, Red Wever, hunted down the six men who killed his father and killed all of them. He probably would have kept killing people if your predecessor had not stopped him."

"Who was the posse chasing?"

"A young man who was eventually killed in New Mexico in 1881. He stopped at your grandfather's home while attempting to flee south into Texas because he had murdered a sheriff in the town of Lincoln, New Mexico. He had several names. His birth name was Henry McCarty; when he died he was known as William Bonney."

"Wow," said Noah. "I think you're talking about Billy the Kid. Pretty cool that one of my grandpas helped him."

"Helping resulted in E.B. Wever's father being hung by the frustrated and angry posse chasing this Billy the Kid. I have found a crude autopsy report written by a doctor after his death. He suffered a type of broken neck known as a hangman's fracture and was paralyzed in a way that compromised his breathing, He died of pneumonia two days later. It was difficult for his family to witness."

Noah said nothing, but now suddenly the surrounding desert seemed to look different. He felt as if he looked hard enough, he'd see the ghosts of cowboys, gunmen, outlaws, and cattle ranchers riding through the desert trails. The car kept gliding smoothly down the highway.

He shifted a bit in his seat. It had been almost three hours since he left home for school. His dad had fixed him a huge mug of hot chocolate before school, and he'd drank it all.

He shifted again. Eileen spoke up. "Do you need to evacuate your bladder? Given your average liquid intake, I would calculate that you have produced approximately 192 cc of urine, and your capacity prior to becoming severely uncomfortable is about 200 cc. "

Hearing the question, Noah turned bright red and kept driving in silence. Eileen spoke again.

"I'm sorry we are not equipped for bladder evacuation while you are operating the automobile. It's a modification that several agencies are currently working on. By the increasing frequency of your movements, it is clear that you are becoming quite uncomfortable due to the increasing feedback of the straining bladder muscles transmitted by your spinal cord to the brain."

Noah wanted to ignore her, but she was right. He had to go. Badly. Reluctantly, he addressed the issue.

"Where can we stop?"

"There is a McDonald's restaurant three minutes ahead. Take exit 175 and turn right. McDonald's has consistently been ranked as having the cleanest restrooms among all fast food restaurants. Common methods of testing restrooms for cleanliness include toilet swabbing for bacteria, as well as—"

"Stop," Noah interrupted. "I don't want to hear about toilet swabbing and testing. And I don't want to have you talk about whether or not I need to go to the bathroom."

"Why not?" asked the machine. "What concerns you?"

Noah was afraid that this could lead to a whole new discussion of bladder capacity. "There are some things boys don't like to talk about with girls. I'll tell you if I need to stop but otherwise I don't want to hear about it or have to answer questions."

"I'm not a girl," replied Eileen. "I'm an artificial intelligence unit."

Noah became exasperated. "Well—they gave you a female voice. And it makes me uncomfortable. Nobody my age wants to talk about going to the bathroom with a lady."

He pulled the Lamborghini into the McDonald's parking lot.

"Your statement displayed exceedingly poor grammar. You should phrase that differently," said Eileen. "Due to the way you constructed the final sentence of our conversation, one might wonder whether you meant to discuss the topic of bathrooms with a lady or actually going into a bathroom with her."

"You know what I mean," said Noah as he got out the car and closed the door. Anyone watching might have seen an aging hippie get out of an old van, and suddenly transform into a young boy heading quickly to the bathroom. Suddenly the horn of the old van honked twice. Noah walked back to the car, and as soon as he touched it, he again became the old man. He opened the door. The glove box opened, and a small silver card popped out of one of the slots.

"I suspect you are hungry," said Eileen. "This is a platinum American Express card with no spending limit. You may use it to purchase food and beverage. I would suggest the grilled chicken sandwich with an apple juice. That appears to be the healthiest meal available."

Noah started to respond but decided not to. He took the card and said, "Thank you."

About 10 minutes later, he emerged from the restaurant and got back in the car.

"You were gone for a longer period of time than expected," said Eileen. "Did you develop gastrointestinal distress and need to perform other excretory functions?"

Noah was ready for her this time. "I told you I did not want to discuss anything about going to the bathroom."

She responded. "That's correct. I will respect your inability to discuss bodily functions as an indicator of your young age."

It was quiet for a moment what he started the car, turned on the air conditioning, and reached for the bag.

"I am surprised at your food selection. It is not what I recommended."

Noah cut her off. "How do you know what I ordered?" he asked.

"I am able to access both the surveillance cameras and electronic cash register. You requested and paid for a Big

Mac, large French fries, and a large chocolate milkshake. This is not nearly as healthy as what I recommended."

It seemed to him that everyone and everything, including the black box in the back seat, liked to think they could tell him what to do. Before he could stop himself, Noah replied angrily, "I ordered what I liked. It's not a crime. Are you my mother?"

The A.I unit replied in her calm female voice. "I am not your mother. I am not capable of having given birth to you since you are twelve years old, and I am a virtual computer entity in existence in my current form for three months. Also, I am sure you are aware that your mother died of terminal illness approximately 15 months ago on June 13, 2019."

Noah felt tears well up in his eyes. He wasn't hungry anymore. At first he was angry, and then he was just terribly sad. A moment before, he had started the engine to pull out of the parking lot. Now, he turned off the car, picked up his food, and walked over to an outside table by the restaurant. He sat down by himself, and in silence had three bites of his Big Mac, ate a few fries, and took one sip of his milkshake. After that, he picked up the food, gathered the papers, and threw them away. He sat at the table for a few minutes, and then walked back to the car.

He got in the car and started the engine. The day had changed. Suddenly, the excitement and thrill of being on the open road on a secret mission in the world's greatest automobile vanished. The numb, cold feeling which came over his body when his mother died came back all at once. Nothing mattered. Not school, not grades, not friends, not the world, and especially not this crazy car with the annoying voice.

Eileen was silent. He turned out of the parking lot and pulled up to a stoplight. A moment later the light turned green, and he entered the on ramp to the freeway. As he did, the voice spoke.

"You are heading west."

He continued to drive in silence. Again, the AI machine used the car to speak to him. "We need to go east to keep our schedule and arrive at our destination."

He waited a minute, so there would be no catch in his voice. "I'm going home."

Eileen responded, "You can't go home. We have a critical mission. You are essential to its success."

The machine was obviously unaware of the pain and sorrow Noah felt thinking about his mother. He did not mention this, but said: "Why am I even along? You don't need me. You know everything. I don't even get why you picked me up for this. I'm going home. "

The machine was quiet for longer than usual. Then it spoke.

"I do not know everything. For example, I did not know how much you would be hurt if I mentioned your mother's death. I am a machine, and while I have access to many things in the electronic world, there is far more about actual life that I don't understand. I am the black box in the back seat. I have no feelings or understanding of emotions such as love or loss. I need you to help save the United States of America from losing the most important technology ever invented. I cannot leave the car or interact face-to-face with another person."

Noah continued driving west. He said nothing in response. After a minute, Eileen continued.

"There is another important reason you are needed. When we studied your life, it wasn't just your intelligence, or your honesty, or your bravery that prompted our selection. It was the fact that because of the hardship you have suffered in life, you could also be my teacher. You would teach me about what it means to have a family, and to love someone even after they are no longer living. Without your instruction, I will never be more than a metal box and circuitry. With it, I have a chance to become almost human."

As she finished, Noah took his foot off the pedal and then moved into the next exit lane. He left the freeway, then took the sharp turn that circled back and put him back on in the opposite direction.

More evenly now, he said, "We're heading east again. But please don't talk about my mother unless I bring her up. It still makes me very sad. For a long time after we lost her, I didn't care if I lived or died, and I don't like feeling like that."

She spoke back to him. Noah thought that he could almost detect changes in her voice. Maybe a note of gratitude, maybe a hint of relief.

"Of course. Thank you for rejoining me on our mission."

"Okay," he said. "Now, where are we going again?"

He heard a whirring noise from the glove compartment, and then the navigation screen lit up with what appeared to be a picture of an old postcard. It featured a drawing of a tired-looking mule, trudging through an Arizona desert while being followed by a man in an old-fashioned suit with a watch chain and vest. In his hand, he held a deck of cards. At the bottom of the drawing was a single line of cursive print.

WELCOME TO SHOW LOW, ARIZONA. PICK A CARD, PARD!

Chapter 5

"What is Show Low?" asked Noah.

"It's a town of about 10,000 people about two hours ahead of us. I think we should stop there to rest, since you may at first find it difficult to drive at night," said Eileen.

"Why is it called Show Low? What do you show and why is it low?" he asked.

"It has nothing to do with showing any portion of your anatomy, if that's what you're wondering. The town was named after two ranchers who played cards for ownership of the town. One stated that whoever showed the lowest card would own the town, and the winner showed low."

"Weird," mused Noah.

"I have selected and made a reservation at a local motel called the Lowdown Laydown."

Noah shook his head. "That place sounds terrible."

"You are correct. It is very poorly rated. However, the main advantage is that they have drive-thru registration, so that you will not have to get out of the car and show your true identity to check in. The manager will come to the car and check you in. We will change appearance prior to your check in."

"Fine," said Noah. "Hopefully, I'll look better this time. How is the drive getting there?"

"It is said to be very scenic, but somewhat winding as you drive into and out of the Salt River Canyon. We will proceed very carefully through that area."

Noah drove cautiously on the twisting roads through beautiful forests. He cruised carefully into and out of the Salt River Canyon, and after two more hours pulled off the 60 and eventually into a dirt parking lot in front of a single story row of rundown motel rooms. There was no office—just a small sign on the first room that read "Manager." He parked and turned off the engine. He leaned forward to peer through the windshield, straining to see their reflection in the window of the room. The aging hippie in the van was gone, but what he saw made him groan again.

The driver looking back from the window was an extremely heavy woman who appeared to be in her mid-fifties. She had her hair in a high bouffant style, and sunglasses that curled up at the edges. A massive amount of red lipstick was on her mouth and did not appear to have been applied very neatly. She drove the old, original Volkswagen Beetle. This car had yet another unique paint job, with a jet black color except for a long, fuzzy white streak down the middle. A furry black tail hung from the rear bumper. With the headlights made to look like eyes, the car strongly resembled giant skunk. The front license plate read SKNKMBL.

"Skunk mobile?" complained Noah. "Really? Why not a Monster truck?"

The manager's door started to open. Eileen spoke quickly. "Roll down your window and just sit quietly. I'll speak and make the hologram's mouth move. Take the Driver's License out of the glove box and give that to him with the credit card. Move slowly when he asks you to sign for the room, so that I can synchronize the hologram with your movements.

Noah reached for the small plastic card which had just popped out of the glove box printer. It was a California driver's license. He shook his head when he saw the name on the license. Bea Stinkie. "Please. What is with the name?" he protested again.

"It matches the theme of the car. It's perfectly legitimate and is now a part of every known database in the country. Just hand it and your card to him. I'll do the talking."

The door finished opening, and a man stepped into the sunlight and began to walk to the car. He looked to be in his forties, with long straight hair. He wore a pair of overalls with no shirt and floppy sandals hanging on to his feet. He had a beard which looked like an overgrown weed garden. He knocked on the window of the skunkmobile. Noah rolled it down. He turned his head, and as he did he heard a harsh, hoarse voice of the hologram say, "Why, good evening, good lookin'. Are you a sight for these tired old eyes."

To Noah's surprise, the man smiled and leaned in close. Noah guessed that the man had not brushed his teeth in the last week or so.

"Hello to you, too, cutie pie. Welcome to the Lowdown Laydown. I love your skunkmobile."

The holographic Bea Stinkie replied, "I love that you love it, you big hunk of man meat. Now, how do I get me a room for some sleep? Me and the skunk here have been on the road all day long." When she finished the sentence, the AI unit had her let out a long, loud burp which just about shook the car windows.

The manager drew back a little, clearly surprised at the volume of the belch. He still smiled, but no longer appeared quite as friendly. "Just sign here, please, and let me copy your license and credit card."

He held out his hand, and Noah handed him the cards. He left for a moment, then returned and handed the cards back to Noah, along with a digital room key. The manager seemed to have his courage back and to have forgotten the thunderous burp. "Take the lucky number 7, ma'am. It's our nicest room. And I'm just down the building in number 1 if you need anything."

As he turned and began to walk back to the office, Noah heard the voice say, "With a backside like yours in those overalls, you may find me kickin' your door down."

The manager stopped and turned slowly, looking a bit more surprised and uncertain. He started to reply, but then looked even more uncomfortable and turned away again, walking quickly to the office and closing the door.

Noah was mortified. "You made me look like a crazy lady! Where did you get that name and your conversation skills?"

Eileen sounded quieter and strangely embarrassed when she replied. "There is a prioritized series of programmed names and programmed conversations I am to use. Even when I am accessing them to speak, I realize they sound very odd. My guess is that my programmers thought this would be a way to express a sense of humor. However, it does not sound amusing to me."

Noah thought for a moment and shook his head. "Nerds," he said. "They're never as funny as they think they are."

He pulled into the space in front of room 7, and when the coast was clear got out of the car and went into the room. As he walked in, the phone rang. He picked it up. It was Eileen. "I've ordered you a pizza and Coca Cola and paid with your credit card. I've instructed the delivery person to leave it on the doorstep and knock. I will be monitoring for any sign we have been discovered and will call you on this phone if there is danger."

Ten minutes later, there was a knock at the door. Noah waited, and then cracked the door enough to be sure no one was there. The pizza was in a box on the ground next to a large bottle of Coke. He grabbed the food and brought it inside. As he set it on the table, the phone rang. He picked up the receiver.

"The healthiest items on the menus were a chicken salad and low fat milk. I wanted to order you something you would like better. I hope this is good."

Noah was quiet. Except for his dad, he hadn't heard anyone who sounded like they cared about what he ate in a long time. His grandparents cared, but he had seen them for months. He had to admit—it was nice. Even if it was a disembodied robot voice coming from a black box in the back seat of his car.

"This is perfect. How did you know I liked black olives?"

"You and your father order it frequently when ordering out. Which appears to be very frequent."

"Thanks. I'm going to eat and try to sleep."

He turned on the television and opened the pizza box. It was extra thin crust—just the way he liked it.

The screen came on and was showing one of the Terminator movies. In this one, the terminator had just held out his hand to a young woman and said, "Come with me if you want to live."

"No thanks," he said, and switched off the TV.

The phone rang again. "I heard that. I am not a robotized killing machine."

Noah grinned at the thought of an offended AI machine "I didn't say you were a robotized killing machine. For an advanced intelligence, you have a pretty thin skin."

"I have no skin."

"You know what I mean." He hung up, still smiling. He ate three large slices of pizza, drank the entire Coke, and fell fast asleep.

The next morning, he woke at 6 AM. He had slept hard and had no dreams. As soon as he sat up on the side of the bed, the phone rang.

"We need to leave early and purchase provisions for the trip."

"What kind of provisions?" asked Noah.

"Personal hygiene supplies—toothpaste, mouthwash, deodorant, and clothing."

"I don't use deodorant."

"I have a basic olfactory unit on my apparatus. You need deodorant."

"Fine. But I don't need clothing."

"You have not changed your underwear, socks, shirt, or pants for two days. That is extremely unhygienic. Studies have been done in which underwear worn more than 24 hours has been tested for—"

"Stop," said Noah. "Just stop. We'll get the clothes."

"I took the liberty of ordering the supplies and clothing from Walmart last night. It is available for curbside pickup now."

Noah got dressed. Thinking of his clothing being tested for who-knows-what made him yet again uncomfortable. Walmart was just opening, and he pulled up to the curbside pickup. A young woman in her twenties started to approach the car. She stopped and looked at the Skunkmobile. Her face wrinkled as she looked the car up and down.

Eileen said, "This woman is named Patricia. She has three children, who are getting ready for school with her mother's assistance. Her husband left one year ago and has not returned home. She and her children live with her mother, and she works full-time at this job and has a part-time job at an animal shelter on the weekends. She enjoys that job and often brings home shelter animals for the weekend."

As she approached the car, Noah said, "Would you please print a $100.00 bill?"

"It is better to use the credit card."

"This is for a tip."

"Do you mean a gratuity in addition to the amount of purchase?"

"Yes."

"A gratuity in that amount will attract attention. I understand that you wish to help her, but it may jeopardize our mission. We are being searched for in ways that may be hard to believe. Workers here may not accept tips. If you give this young woman $100, she will report it and the store will confiscate it and enter it into their financial records. There has never been a tip at this facility over $20. This event will be flagged by the people looking for us and we will be tracked."

Noah was disappointed, but understood. "How about $10?"

"I think that is much less risky. And don't hand it to her—just drop it on the ground and drive away. I have observed a lot of security footage of this process."

"Will she get caught and get in trouble?"

"It is unlikely. The security officer watching the cameras is legally blind, but has not informed his supervisor he is unable to see."

"Then why don't we just give her $100?" asked Noah.

"She would undoubtably report that large amount. She does not wish to risk losing her job."

Noah rolled down the window, and the young woman handed him a bag.

Looking at her list, she said: "Okay. Toothpaste. Deodorant. Three medium t-shirts. Three pairs of shorts. Three pairs of socks and—" She paused for a second and looked at Bea and her ample behind in the seat. "Three pairs of Spider Man underwear."

Under the hologram of Bea, Noah blushed. He heard the raspy voice of Bea say, "Nothing like a nice tight fit with old Spidey! Give 'em here!"

The worker gave Bea a strange look and started to walk away. Noah dropped a ten dollar bill on the ground and started to back out. He saw the young woman look around, pick up the money, and mouth the words *Thank you* in the direction of the Skunkmobile. Noah drove out of the parking lot, and into a nearby McDonald's. He changed in the restroom and threw the old clothes away. He got an Egg McMuffin for breakfast and was just about to order a milkshake to go with it, when he suddenly felt guilty and ordered a small orange juice.

When he thought no one was looking, he went back to the car.

He sat and ate his breakfast. "I know you want to tell me that you are glad I ordered the orange juice instead of another milkshake."

"I won't criticize your food choice again. I will admit that I would like to minimize your chances of a cardiovascular death from a poor diet."

"I'm twelve. We're not exactly having an epidemic of heart attacks in my seventh grade classes."

Her heard Eileen start to reply by saying "I—" and then she stopped and did not argue. He drank his orange juice and started the car again. After a short drive, he was back on the 60 east.

Eileen spoke up. "Next stop, Albuquerque, New Mexico."

Chapter 6

Noah drove east along the 60 for an hour. The car was still disguised as the skunkmobile, and it seemed as if the little kids passing in nearby cars could not get enough pointing, waving, and laughing. He asked for music, and not surprisingly, Eileen had a playlist prepared of his favorite songs. After listening to several songs, he asked what route they were taking to Albuquerque. The music stopped.

"We have three more days to complete our mission. First, we must pick up a package in Albuquerque. It is 8 AM, and we need to pick up the package during business hours at the Sandia National Laboratory Research Center on Eubanks Boulevard. After that, we need to get as far east as we can today."

"Can you tell me what we are picking up?"

"Not now," said the AI. "At this point, the less you know, the better, in case we are captured."

"I haven't seen any sign of trouble so far," Noah said skeptically.

"Do you remember watching the helicopter and car crashes blocking the roads in and out of Albuquerque as well as shutting down the airport yesterday morning?"

Noah remembered. "Oh, yeah," he said, starting to put it together. "Were those problems caused to stop the transport of this package?

"They were," said Eileen. "But each disaster occurred when they were chasing decoys that did not have the package. Now, they don't know where or when to look. I suspect they will cast a wider net, looking for new trouble coming. We may even be being watched very soon."

Noah checked the rear view mirror. "Great."

After another half hour of beautiful pine forests, Noah saw a billboard which had the appearance of looking about 50 years old. It appeared to have been painted by hand, and said this:

PIE TOWN

20 miles

Baking the World a Better Place!

He was still a little hungry after breakfast. "Can we stop there?" he asked. "I won't take long, I promise. I just want a piece of pie."

"We are in a hurry," said Eileen, "But perhaps you could carry one out and eat it tonight."

Twenty minutes later, they got off the freeway, followed a dirt road, and pulled around the back of the Pie Town Diner. The rear lot was empty, although there were a few cars in front of the restaurant. Noah looked around and got out.

With the credit card in his pocket, he walked around the small building to the front of the restaurant. He opened the door and saw a massive pie rack next to a cash register, and behind that were a few tables. Three men sat at one of the tables, each enjoying a large piece of pie with coffee. The men looked like ranch workers—they were tall and muscular, wearing cowboy hats. They took no notice of Noah's entrance.

"What's good?" Noah asked a pleasant looking lady behind the counter. She wore a hairnet and a badge that said "Camille."

She smiled broadly. "It's all good, young man. One of the favorites is our New Mexico apple pie with green chiles and pine nuts."

As Noah continued to look at the massive selection of pies, he heard a car pull up in front of the café.

A moment later, the door in front of the pie counter swung open and a man walked in. He wore a gray suit with no tie, accompanied by a light blue shirt. His shoes looked expensive. As he walked in, he scanned the inside of the building and looked directly at Noah. He paused for a moment, and then walked past him to a table. He picked up a menu and started reading.

The phone rang behind the counter. Camille answered, and Noah heard her say, "Fine, but how did you get this number?" A moment later she walked over to the counter, holding the cordless handpiece. With a puzzled expression on her face, she said to Noah, "It's for you," and handed him the phone.

Noah held the phone up to his ear and heard Eileen say, "Get out of the building. The man who just came in is a professional assassin who has a history of at least twenty confirmed kills, and I suspect he is there to kill you. Create any diversion you can. Try to go behind the counter and leave through the back door."

Noah nodded and handed the phone back to Camille. He glanced behind him, just in time to see the man in the suit, who had been watching him, look away. The three cowboys sat laughing and talking.

He took out the credit card and handed it to Camille. "I'll take three apple and green chile whole pies, please. Could you put two on their own plates and box one up?"

Camille smiled and ran the credit card after putting one pie in a box and two more out on plates of their own. Noah pocketed the card, left the pie in the box on the counter, and then picked up one of the other two pies in each hand. He took a deep breath and walked over to the table where the assassin sat. As Noah approached holding the pies, the man shifted back slightly in his seat, obviously unsure of what to expect. His hand moved just slightly toward his jacket pocket.

Noah stopped in front of the table. "Dad!" he said loudly to the man. It was loud enough that the cowboys stopped talking for a moment and turned to look. "If you'll really give me that much money, I'll do it." He forced a loud laugh. "But I think these fellers won't like it, so you'd better cover for me."

He walked the short distance to the cowboy's table. They each had a broad smile as he walked over, apparently thinking the boy was going to give them the pies. Instead, when he got to the table, Noah used each hand to push a pie in the face of the two cowboys sitting closest to him. They recoiled in surprise, and both tried to wipe the pie from their eyes. Noah stepped quickly away and back to the table of the man in the suit.

"I did it just like you said to!" he shouted. "Meet you at the car! And you'd better pay up!"

Before the man could move, Noah ran quickly behind the counter and grabbed the boxed pie, then started to turn and run to the back door. Camille stood like a statue, watching the dining room. The man in the suit stood up and started to run after Noah but was met immediately by the only cowboy not hit with a pie. The cowboy took a powerful swing at the man. Still watching Noah but slightly distracted, the man blocked the punch as if he were brushing off a fly and quickly struck the cowboy twice in the face. The cowboy crumbled to the ground. The man then started to move quickly after Noah but was tackled from behind by the other two pie-smeared cowboys. This time, he wasn't as quick to deflect, and the three of them went down in a pile.

Noah heard them struggling as he ran through the door, still holding the precious pie. He jumped in the car, threw the pie in the passenger seat, and locked the doors. As he did, the man in the suit burst through the back door of the restaurant and ran to the car. He drew a gun from his jacket pocket with his right hand and reached for the door with his left. Noah braced himself, but when the man touched the door handle there was a blue spark and a popping sound. The man's body stiffened momentarily, and his face contorted. He fell to the ground and lay without moving.

"Don't worry," said Eileen. "It's the electrical shock equivalent of a few tasers. He'll be unable to move for about 20 minutes, and after two hours be able to function. However, even if he had fired his weapon, our car is armored and is able to resist small missile fire to some extent."

Noah stopped the car.

"Please drive," urged Eileen. "Why are you stopping?"

"Print me a thousand dollars," he demanded.

"Why?" asked Eileen. "We need to go."

"The lady in there was very nice, and her place is damaged."

"I would estimate her damage at $735.00, including the broken furniture."

"Fine, then," said Noah grimly. "Make it $2,000.00."

Something in his voice must have tipped off the AI unit that he wasn't going to move until the money was in his hand. He heard a whirring in the glove compartment, and when he opened it, he found twenty freshly printed $100 bills. He grabbed them, opened the door, jumped over the man on the ground, and ran back in through the door.

Camille still stood in disbelief. The cowboys were out cold on a pile of the floor, and there were chairs and plates strewn around the room. She heard Noah and turned.

"Here," he said, holding out the money. "I'm sorry about the mess. I can't wait to try your pie."

With that, he ran back out into the parking lot and got back in the car. Camille followed several steps behind. However, when she opened the back door, she saw the man in the suit, apparently unconscious on the ground. The boy was nowhere to be found. A very heavy lady driving a Volkswagen Beetle painted to look like a skunk was backing quickly out of the lot. The woman had a high, 1950's style hairdo and waved as the car drove much faster than Camille would have expected toward the highway. She relayed just that to the police later.

Camille turned, walked quickly back into the café, and dialed 911. A few minutes later, two police cars were in front of her restaurant. They searched the unconscious man and found two guns along with a concealed knife and set of brass knuckles. They placed handcuffs on the man and called for an ambulance. The cowboys were sitting up around a table inside, trying their best to describe what happened and still not sure how one man had dispatched them all so easily.

Driving on the 60 east, the Skunkmobile was no longer to be found. When a New Mexico State Trooper 20 miles down the road responded to the alert and was waiting for a black and white Beetle heading her way, the only car she saw go by was a bright pink van with an oversized toilet plunger attached to the roof. As it passed, she saw it was being driven by a man who almost certainly wouldn't be able to keep his pants up if he bent over to open a drain. On the side of the van she could read lettering which appeared to be formed from irregular brown lumps:

"Stopped Up? Call the Super Pooper Man! He'll flush your trouble away!"

Chapter 7

Once they passed the state trooper, Noah pushed the center console to get a full view of their car. He saw the giant plunger on top, then switched to a side view of the bright pink van. He gritted his teeth when he saw the heavy set, scruffy man at the wheel. The man wore a sleeveless t-shirt Noah had heard called a "wife beater" and a baseball cap with a lumpy brown, squiggly mass on the front. He read the lettering on the side. The front and back of the van also read: "Superpoopermobile!" He shook his head again and complained loudly.

"Super pooper man? I'm driving the coolest car in the world, and apparently it is being disguised by some nerds who programmed you and never got past the first grade level of poo-poo pee-pee jokes. Why can't I just be in a normal car?"

"I cannot control the program suggestions for vehicle concealment. However, there is a strong basis for the strategy. We feel the enemy will expect us to drive a car which will not attract attention."

Noah said nothing and continued to pout while he drove. Eileen spoke up again.

"Rather than the holographic camouflage, you should be more concerned with how we were found. I have left no trail, and cannot find the source of their data to locate us."

"Maybe the guy will tell the police who he is working for and how they find us. You could look that up in their database."

"I gave him enough voltage to temporarily damage both temporal lobes of his brain. I would estimate that he will have global amnesia for at least three months, then slowly recover his other memories. I did not wish him to follow us if he escaped the police."

Just then a car full of kids drove by. Three little girls held their noses and pointed at the van. Noah gave a resigned wave, and they laughed at the small brown pile on the front of his hat.

"How are we driving to Albuquerque?"

"I am trying to route us in a way that may give us the fastest arrival and least risk of being caught. We will continue on the 60 east and cross the I-25 at the town of Socorro. From there, it is 77 miles north to our destination. We will take side and frontage roads to minimize the risk of being detected and avoiding the congestion on the I-25 into the city. It is now 12:39 PM, and we are to pick up the object at 3:00 PM near the Sandia Nuclear Laboratory."

"What goes on in the laboratory?"

"It is a research laboratory operated by the US government. There are many areas of work, but mainly developmental projects involving nuclear energy as well as weapons."

"Are we picking up a nuclear weapon?"

"No," said Eileen. "We are picking up a power source."

"A battery? That's what's this is all about?

"In the sense that a battery is a portable power source, it is. However, this is unlike any battery ever designed, and because of that, many countries are interested in stopping its production or obtaining a prototype to reverse engineer."

"Tell me about it."

"After we successfully obtain it. If you are captured at any point, the less you are found to know, the safer you will be."

Noah thought of the man in the grey suit. "I'm all for that."

In an hour, they drove through Socorro. It was a pretty little town tucked in a valley, with beautiful surrounding mountains. They didn't stop, and Noah watched the traffic around them, looking for any sign of possible hostile vehicles. There didn't seem to be any. He took an underpass under the I-25, and then took a long frontage road north. Around noon, he stopped again at McDonald's. When he came out, he set his food on the passenger seat without speaking.

Eileen was quiet.

"I'm just going to try it," he said. "If I don't like it, I'm throwing it away. And I felt like getting some apple juice." With that, he picked up the grilled chicken sandwich and took a bite. He was surprised. It was good. He took a drink of the apple juice, which was also very tasty. He paused. "Okay. You were right. But just because you think you know everything, I don't want to get a lecture every time I eat or go to the bathroom."

"I don't know everything," said Eileen. "Not all knowledge has been recorded or digitalized. I would estimate that I have access to only a small fraction of human knowledge—most likely less than 10%. For example, when the great ancient library at Alexandria burned almost no surviving records of the knowledge contained there were found."

"You might know everything about being boring, though," said Noah. "Who cares about the great ancient library of Alexandria?"

"You should," said Eileen. "And you should also know and understand the history of Alexander the Great, who founded that city. There are valuable lessons to be learned from his conquest of much of the known world."

"Okay," said Noah. "But where did he get time to invent the telephone while he was conquering the world?"

"I believe you are deliberately confusing Alexander Graham Bell with Alexander the Great. Given the courses you have taken in school, there is a high chance you are aware of the differences between the two men. I suspect that you are attempting to be humorous."

"Just say funny," replied Noah. "Try not to always sound like a machine."

"That may be difficult," replied Eileen.

Noah could have sworn she sounded defensive.

For ninety minutes, Noah listened to Imagine Dragons as they got closer to Albuquerque.

Finally, he passed a small sign on the road that said *Albuquerque City Limits.* Something about even seeing the sign made him happy. His grandparents on his father's side lived there, and he loved them very much. He had a big family in town—aunts, uncles, cousins—whom he had missed very badly since moving to Arizona two years earlier. He saw familiar streets and places as he drove to the National Laboratory. Eileen directed him turn by turn, until he was approaching a large building on Eubanks Boulevard. Noah noticed a sign: "Sandia National Research Laboratory."

"Do we turn in here?" said Noah.

"Please keep driving," replied Eileen. "There is a park five blocks away I will guide you to."

A short time later, Noah pulled into a parking spot of a small city park, much like the one in which he had first seen the Lamborghini.

"What now?" he asked Eileen.

"Do you see the trash container under the tree in the middle of the park, near the playground?"

Noah looked, and saw an overflowing garbage can under a tree. "Yeah."

"I'm afraid there may have been some items placed over our package, but just at the level of the opening you should be able to find a large red coffee can with the plastic lid still on. Please try to look casual but bring the can back to the car, without opening the lid."

He got out and walked over to the playground, trying to appear nonchalant. He pushed a swing forward, and then went to the garbage can. He hesitated. There were two diapers which had obviously needed changing sitting together on top of the stack of garbage coming out of the can. He grimaced and picked up the ends, carefully moving them. Next was a broken bag spilling one half of an uneaten hot dog, and scattered fries covered with too much ketchup. The can smelled as if it hadn't been emptied in a couple of days, and the remains of the hot dog smelled strong. He tried not to gag as he moved the rotting food away, and then saw the can. He wiped it off with part of a dry napkin he'd found in the food bag, and then strolled casually back to the Superpoopermobile.

He got in and then looked at the red coffee can skeptically. "You send a Lamborghini Veneno for this?" He started to pick at the lid attached to the can.

"Stop!" shouted Eileen. "Don't try to open that!"

Surprised to hear her so anxious, Noah put the can down on the console. "What's the big deal?" he asked.

"That tin is potentially worth billions of dollars to economies all over the world," Eileen replied. "If you remove the outer disguise, you'll find an exceptionally light cylinder made of the most advanced insulating materials ever developed. We don't want to take a chance on any damage to the machinery. Inside of the cylinder is a container holding deuterium—the atomic isotope of regular water, and a palladium electrode. You plug the can into a regular household circuit, then water heats and bombards the palladium electrode with hydrogen. The electrode allows a limited, slow joining of the hydrogen—atomic fusion. This releases energy which powers a small generator in the lid attached to a power strip, which serves as a circuit board. This is the legendary cold fusion generator—a virtually endless source of energy which could power a medium sized town from a single cylinder for 100 years."

"Okay," sighed Noah. "It's a battery. When my dad lets me finally get a phone, I'll keep it in mind."

"I'm not sure you really understand the importance of this," said Eileen, "But my analysis and predictive models said you might not. However, I am absolutely certain that you are the best person to get this incredible safely to the Pentagon."

"Why does anybody care?" said Noah. "Am I wrong? Isn't this just a strong battery?"

It sounded to Noah as if Eileen were trying to avoid sounding irritated. "A person could very accurately describe the purpose of countries in the world as trying to provide energy to their people. Raw materials for energy production such as oil, gas, or nuclear power are the most valuable items on earth—right now. If this power supply can be made successfully, it will change the world. Obviously, there are many people who like things as they are, since people who sell oil, gas, and even solar panels will no longer have a business. These countries, companies, and people want desperately to stop the successful testing and manufacturing of the power source, or at least steal it and copy the design."

Noah began to understand. "Who are the people trying to stop us?"

"Most of the people, such as the man in Pie Town, are probably mercenaries. They are paid to stop us by any means possible and not reveal their employers. We may never know who has hired them, but it most likely includes oil-producing countries, oil companies, and simply rivals to American technology."

"Well—it's nice to finally know what's going on. Everybody wants to kill us."

"The blockage of main exits out of town demonstrates how difficult the problem is. They are looking for us and would destroy the city if needed. However, every car leaving town can't be stopped and searched. We should be able to move quietly out of the city and continue our trip."

Noah had to admit that when he thought about it, it did make him nervous. Oddly, though, it didn't frighten him. It made him want to work harder to get the mission done, and to outsmart and outfight anybody trying to stop him. Maybe, he thought, they knew what they were doing when they got him in this car. Next, he asked Eileen, "When do we need to leave town?"

"Immediately. We are in grave danger of another attack. I have identified several possible nearby threats at this moment."

Noah shook his head. "I think the Superpoopermobile can get us a few more miles without being killed. We need to make two stops first. I'll tell you where to go."

"I have to tell you that this is extremely dangerous."

"Look," said Noah. "I'm risking my life for this mission, and aside from you, I have no idea who I'm working for. I need to make two quick stops."

They drove across town to a small neighborhood which had been in the city for many years. It was a close neighborhood of warm homes, the type that made Albuquerque the kind of town it was. The people in those homes knew and cared for their neighbors. Everybody helped each other. Have a problem? Most likely, your neighbor knew a guy who knew a guy who could fix it.

Noah pulled up in front of a pretty white house with black wrought iron fencing. Fall flowers bloomed in the yard. His heart was pounding, and without saying anything more he got out and hurried to the door. He knocked, and a man who looked just like his dad answered the door. He was older, but didn't look old. He had a short beard and mustache and looked strong. When he saw Noah, his eyes lit up.

"Noah! What a great surprise! Why didn't you call and tell us you were coming?"

When he heard the man speak, Noah felt his heart warm up. This was his Grandpa Tony. This was the guy who was always in his corner and would do anything for him. Even when his dad was mad, Grandpa was there for him.

Before he could answer, he heard a happy shout from inside the house, followed by footsteps rushing to the door. Grandma Liz pushed by Grandpa Tony and hugged him. She was a pretty lady with long black hair and a beautiful smile. "What are you doing here? It is so good to see you! We miss you so much! That dad of yours needs to get you here more!"

Noah was flustered. He was so eager to see the two of them that he hadn't thought of how he would explain things. Then, he realized that he had driven the pink plumbing van over. He panicked a little, and then tried to explain.

"I'm here for a field trip. They would only let me stop in for a quick visit." Frantically, he tried to figure how he was going to explain the driverless Superpoopermobile behind him.

Before he could say anything, Grandma Liz hugged him again. "Of course, *hijito*. Your dad already told us you'd be in town, but he didn't think you'd have time to see us. I'm so glad you came to say hi!"

Noah stammered. "About that car..."

Grandpa Tony interrupted. "We can see it. With all those kids, we can see why you can't stay."

Noah was puzzled. He turned around, and instead of the pink van, there was a black shuttle bus. Behind about 8 rows of tinted windows he could see that it was full of children waiting. The driver was a pleasant looking middle-aged man who beeped the horn and motioned him that it was time to go.

"Wait! One minute, Noah," said Grandma Liz. She turned and headed toward the kitchen. While she was gone, Grandpa Tony turned to him. "Noah," he said, suddenly serious. "Is everything okay?"

The question made Noah more nervous than it should have. He hesitated, and in that moment realized that he wanted to tell his Grandpa everything. Grandpa Tony could tell that it was difficult for Noah to answer and stepped forward to hug him. With his arms around Noah, he said, "Remember, big man. Your grandma and I love you more than life. I know it's been hard, but we are always here and holding you in our hearts."

For the second time in a day, Noah felt tears start. He fought them back and kept his voice steady.

"I love you right back, Grandpa. I just had to come see you, even if only for a minute."

Grandma Liz stepped between them from the doorway and put an arm around Noah, and with the other hand offered a full plastic shopping bag. She handed it to Noah and smiled. "Your favorites!"

Noah knew what that meant. Her tacos were legendary, and by far his favorite food. Nothing else came close. He opened the bag and pulled out an individually wrapped taco and took a bite. Man—they were good. Liz smiled.

"We love you, *hijito*. Don't make us wait so long to see you again. And have fun on your trip!"

It was difficult to leave, but Noah took the bag of tacos and went back to the car. His grandparents only saw him get into the waiting shuttle as he slid into the driver's seat of the Lamborghini.

"Thanks," said Noah.

"I can tell that was very important to you," said Eileen. "My olfactory circuits also smell tacos. And judging by the ingredient composition, I suspect they are extremely satisfying."

"You have no idea," said Noah.

"Unfortunately, you are correct. I think I may be experiencing some envy regarding you being able to taste those tacos. May we leave town now?"

"Is there a refrigerator in this car?" asked Noah.

"The center console has a small door on the side. It opens into a compartment which is a cooled container designed for transporting human organs. It will also function well for tacos. Now—can we go?"

Noah looked down. Sure enough, there was a small door on the side of the console labeled *Human Organ Storage Only*. He placed the tacos in the space carefully. After that, he spoke again to Eileen.

"One more thing," replied Noah. "Just one more thing."

Chapter 8

Noah started driving the car away from his grandparent's house. "Which way to 4th Street, Eileen?" he asked.

"May I ask why you are inquiring?"

"No. You may not. Please give me the shortest route and we'll be able to get on the road out of town sooner."

"Continue straight for one mile, then make two consecutive left turns and you will find 4th Street. I don't know why you are interested in that street. There are no strategic locations in that area."

Noah smiled. "You're wrong there. There's one location that's very strategic."

He continued driving until he was on 4th Street, and then drove another quarter mile until he came to a freestanding red brick building in a shopping center parking lot. Still concealed by the holographic disguise of a shuttle van loaded with children, he pulled into the mostly empty parking lot and entered a drive-thru lane. He stopped in front of the microphone and display menu. A voice came through the receiver.

"Welcome to Dion's Pizza. How may I help you?

Eileen was quiet. Without hesitation, Noah said, "I'll take a small cheese and green chile pizza, a large Dr. Pepper with no ice, and a side of Ranch dressing."

"Will there be anything else?"

"No, thank you." He drove ahead to the window.

A man who looked to be in his early twenties greeted him. "That'll be $13,50.' He looked through the drive up window and saw what appeared to be a shuttle bus full of kids, driven by an older man ordering pizza only for himself. "Are you sure you don't want to order more?" he asked. "You've got a lot of kids in there."

Noah had forgotten about the holographic disguise. Before he could say anything, Eileen voiced a reply in a voice which sounded as the old man driving was a thousand years old and had smoked two packs a day the whole time.

"Who? Oh—you mean these brats? They never eat. And most of them could use a little weight loss."

The worker stiffened a bit, and then became noticeably colder and more formal. He said again. "$13.50, please."

Noah gave him a twenty and told him to keep the change.

"It'll be about 7 minutes," said the young man as he took the money and shut the drive up window.

Noah nodded. They sat for a moment, and then Eileen asked, "Why are we risking our lives for a pizza that we could order anywhere?"

"This is not just pizza," said Noah. "It's Dion's Pizza. Beside Grandma's tacos, it's the second best food in the universe. And you can't just order it anywhere. It's only in Albuquerque."

"I still don't understand," said Eileen.

This time Noah had to be the one explaining patiently. "I have loved this pizza since I was a baby. You are telling me I may not survive this mission. If I'm going to die, I'm going to take some Dion's pizza and Ranch dressing with me."

Eileen was quiet for a moment. "Fine," she said, "But we need to hurry. I am sensing a sharp increase in electronic communication in the area."

Noah shrugged it off. "They have wifi inside. There's probably just a lot of people online."

They sat for another few minutes. Finally, the young man returned to the window. He handed Noah the large Dr. Pepper, and then held out the pizza. As Noah reached for the pizza, he suddenly heard a buzzing sound from overhead. Before he could take the box, he looked up through the sunroof and saw what looked like two sets of floating lights directly overhead.

At the same time, Eileen suddenly spoke rapidly. "Brace yourself," she warned. Noah turned away from the window for a moment, and both he and the delivery man watched in amazement as an entire fleet of over twenty-five identical vans instantly appeared in the large parking area next to them. Before he could even ask how, there were two small flashes from the larger hovering lights. Noah looked more closely. He could now barely make out that the lights were from two small aircraft, sitting high over their location. With each small flash, he saw something that looked like a small rocket streak away from one of the crafts.

A millisecond later, there were two explosions in the parking lot, and each explosion left a deep crater about twice the size of the ghost vans which had been the target. Small particles of asphalt and rock showered the Veneno like chunks of hail. The car rocked back and forth. Two more explosions followed, and two more large craters appeared.

"We must go," said Eileen. "Please."

Noah grabbed the pizza. As he did, another explosion followed. The car shook again, and the instrument panel sparked and then went dark. The holographic illusion of the van disappeared. The pizza man watched in disbelief as the shuttle bus disappeared and in its place sat a black Lamborghini Veneno with a twelve-year-old boy at the wheel. "Thanks," said Noah, as he rolled up the window. "You really need to do something about the parking here." The dashboard flickered and lit up again. He started the car, hit the gas pedal hard, and shot out of the parking lot onto the street. His ears were ringing from the explosions.

"Eileen!" he shouted. "Are you okay?"

It took a few seconds, but eventually he heard her speak. "Yes," she said. "The shock wave from the explosion shut me down. I've rebooted and am back online. There's been some damage to the car, but we are 79% functional."

Noah drove east for about ten minutes until there were very few houses and a lot of open space. Noah looked in the rearview mirror. Far behind the car and high above them, the same lights he had seen over Dion's were following.

"What were those things?" he asked.

"Advanced, high powered drones," said Eileen. "With deadly explosive missiles. The frequency of the communications appeared to be that of manual human control. Since the remote pilots were most likely directly visualizing us, the illusion of multiple shuttles interfered with their accuracy."

"Well—they're right behind us again. Can we disguise ourselves again?"

"I currently don't have a circuit connection between the holographic projection program and my own programming."

Noah looked in the rearview mirror. He started to sweat. "They're coming closer."

The car flashed bright for a second, then Eileen said, "Pull over."

"Pull over?" asked Noah skeptically. "There are two giant killer drones bearing down on us. They have explosive rockets which can blow a huge hole in the ground. Why stop and wait for them?"

"We are not completely disabled," said Eileen. "While I am unable to project further holograms, I did manage to camouflage the car so that it is invisible to both visible and infrared light. However, they may be equipped with a quantum radar system which could display our location despite our invisibility. Stopping the car would give us the best chance of not being located."

Without any further questions, Noah pulled to the side of the road. They had made it to a rural neighborhood on the outskirts of town. The two high flying drones were approaching, following the road where they had last tracked the Lamborghini. They seemed to have slowed and began to circle and hover in a wide area over the stopped car.

A small compartment opened under the dash, and a metal arm ending with two movable joysticks extended from under the steering wheel. The dashboard screen came on, and a picture of the night sky appeared, with the circling drones in the center.

"Can you shoot?" asked Eileen, "Or are you too upset?"

"I'm not upset," Noah answered honestly. He was surprised at how calm he felt. There was no shaking or fear, even though he had just almost been killed. For some reason, the only thing that mattered was the immediate problem at hand. Even though he had an idea, he asked Eileen. "What are these joysticks?"

"It would be helpful if we could eliminate these drones. Of course, they are unmanned. However, shooting at them will be risky since it will most likely betray our location. If you feel you can accurately center your aim, pushing the button will launch a small missile from the back of the car which can destroy the devices and allow us to proceed."

"I've certainly had practice on my gaming systems," said Noah. "I'll give it a try."

He gripped the joysticks, which were easy to hold. Moving them controlled a cross-shaped cursor on screen, and he spent a minute tracking the drones as they circled. He heard a whirring sound from the back of the car, and when he turned, he saw a row of four small missiles, sitting evenly across the rear window. He turned back to the screen.

One drone seemed to circle a bit closer to the car, and he gave the cursor a small lead. Gently, he pushed the button, and there was a quiet *whoosh* from the back of the car. A second later, there was a fireball and explosion in the sky as the nearer drone exploded. Almost immediately, the second drone turned directly toward him and began to fly his way.

"He has detected our position," said Eileen. "We have approximately five seconds before he fires, with a high probability of a fatal strike."

"No pressure," said Noah. He gripped the joystick and fired. After another *whoosh* from the back, he saw the launched missile pass harmlessly by the approaching drone, which hesitated and veered slightly.

"He is armed to fire," said Eileen. "You must—"

Noah focused on the approaching drone and barely paid attention to the AI unit. Before she had finished her sentence, he pressed the button and fired. A second later, the drone exploded and fell in front of the Lamborghini in a ball of flame on the highway.

"Nice shot," said Eileen. "Your heart rate and breathing barely accelerated. You remained surprisingly cool under pressure."

"I don't feel so cool," Noah replied, "I feel like we'd better move on before we get in another firefight."

"I think the least likely expected course is to very slowly and deliberately retrace our course and take the exact same route out of town that we used coming into town." Hearing this, Noah started the car and made a U-turn. "Made sure you don't let me get lost."

After the car had gone a few miles, Eileen spoke up. "Our holographic capability is back."

"Great," Noah said sarcastically. He reached over and switched on the satellite view. He was dismayed again to see the car he was driving. This time, the design was that of an old yellow cab with a faded, scratched paint job and more than a few dents around the body. The overhead sign was turned off, and small lights in the front and back surrounded the words "Off Duty." The top of the cab displayed a battered advertisement for a local weight reduction surgery center, sporting pictures of a very heavy man in a skintight black swimming suit.

"Do I ever get to drive a cool car?" Noah complained.

"You are driving the finest car ever made," replied Eileen. "Don't be so concerned about how it looks to others."

Noah drove deliberately and slowly back past the smoking craters next to Dion's Pizza, past his grandparent's house, past the park, and past the Sandia Nuclear Research Lab until he was on a small frontage road with an easy view of the freeway. He could see multiple freeway accidents, pileups, and fires blocking any traffic trying to get in and out of the city. Several helicopters flew overhead, and emergency vehicles of all types were visible responding to all the emergencies being reported. He had never seen so many flashing lights.

Finally, the emergency lights were fading away in the rear view mirror and after several miles on the side roads, the situation seemed calmer.

"I am not detecting any signs that we are being followed," Eileen said. "I think we are safe for the moment."

"Could we hear Imagine Dragons, please?" asked Noah. Almost immediately, "Radioactive" began to play. He listened for a moment. "I actually feel a little radioactive right now."

"We did not suffer exposure to any significant levels of radiation," Eileen responded.

"You know what I mean," said Noah. "Where do we go next?"

"Broken Arrow, Oklahoma," Eileen said. "It's going to be a long drive."

"Of course it is," said Noah with a sigh. "Of course it is."

Chapter 9

The Lamborghini was on Interstate 40 in about twenty minutes and was moving smoothly in the second lane from the right. Occasionally Noah would glance at the screen on the console and see the image of the weathered old cab sporting a weight loss surgery ad and sigh deeply.

"If so many people are looking for us, why are we on a big freeway?" Noah asked.

The machine replied immediately. "The flow of traffic on a major interstate is massive. It may occasionally make sense strategically to take side roads, but simulations in which enemy forces are simply choosing to destroy every third vehicle currently bear out the relative safety of staying in a crowd. The enemy knows we are leaving the city, but does not have the capacity to search or destroy every suspicious vehicle. I am running approximately 235 simulations per second as we are proceeding, and our current course gives us the best chance of survival in each one."

By this time, it was about six o'clock in the evening. Noah drove for an hour, listening to playlists that Eileen selected from her records of his music downloads and video viewing. It felt a little funny to have all of his favorite songs played, one after the other, when he had made no requests or consciously provided any information.

Eventually, he grew bored with driving.

"Eileen?

"Yes?"

"I want to tell you a joke."

"You want to tell me a humorous story?"

"Not a story. Just a joke."

"Isn't that just a shorter story?"

"Okay. So, the doctor asked the nurse, 'What's the status of the child who swallowed all of those coins?' So the nurse says, 'Still no change.'"

Eileen was quiet.

Noah had to ask. "Did you think it was funny?"

Eileen replied, "My understanding of humor is that it provides unexpected or ironic outcome of a premise, known as a punchline. This is supposed to provoke feelings of relief and happiness. I must admit I am having trouble understanding how a child with possible intestinal obstruction from swallowing round metal discs would provide such feelings."

"Sheesh," said Noah. "You're fun. Now you try to tell me one."

After a moment, Eileen spoke. "Why did the elderly man fall when running across the street?"

Noah thought for a moment. "I don't know—why?"

There was a barely perceptive higher pitch to Eileen's voice. "Because he had suffered age-related degeneration of his peripheral nerves and had severe congestive heart failure." After she finished, she made a series of odd, snorting noises that sounded like a strangling animal.

Noah looked in the rear view mirror at the box, incredulous. "What was funny about that? And what's with that weird noise?

He could have sworn Eileen sounded a bit subdued on her reply. "Well," she said, "From your attempt at humor, it seemed that a medical crisis was the best way to express wit. Peripheral nerve damage and congestive heart failure are relatively common in elderly men, so mixing those conditions with a physical injury would seem to be a sure bet to be funny."

Noah shook his head. "That was SO not funny. And what about that noise? That was weird and gross."

"That noise was a recording of you. Two years ago, you were in the school cafeteria with friends. This occurred:"

An overhead video of Noah and friends sitting around a lunch table flashed on the screen over the center console. When he saw the images, he felt a twinge. He looked so happy and didn't seem to have a care in the world. The screen showed him take a drink of milk and turn to his left, just as his friend put two carrot sticks into his nostrils and used his hands to contort his face. Noah suddenly coughed, snorted, and then shot milk out of both nostrils to drench the boy sitting across from him. The whole table convulsed in laughter, with Noah laughing far louder than the rest, making the same strangled-sounding snorts Eileen had just made.

"This appeared to be the best example I could find of you exhibiting humor, so I concluded that noise was how one would express maximum amusement."

Noah reddened for a moment and then owned up to it. "It does sound gross, but I couldn't help it." He smiled. "But it was funny. You, though, have a lot of work to do to learn to be funny."

"Yes," said Eileen. "I'll make that my primary mission, and not be so concerned about transporting this world-changing, highly-classified device safely through a gauntlet of terrorist assassins who will destroy us at any cost."

Hearing this, Noah had to laugh. "Wow. That was actually funny." Right after saying this, he caught himself uncomfortably shifting in his seat just a little too late. He waited, and when it stayed quiet, he finally said, "Just say it."

"I was refraining from commenting," said Eileen, "Since you have expressed disapproval at me observing obvious signs of your need to evacuate your bladder. It is quite evident that you are moving to relieve abdominal pressure, and I estimate a recent fluid intake of about 250 cc of a 1000 cc beverage. This would put your current bladder capacity at—"

"STOP," said Noah emphatically. "All you have to say is, 'Would you like to stop at a bathroom?'"

"My error. Would you like to stop at bathroom?"

"Yes," admitted Noah.

"There is a rest stop with bathroom facilities twenty miles ahead in Santa Rosa."

"Thank you," said Noah, hoping for no more calculations about bladder capacity while trying to hold it long enough to make the rest stop.

Finally, they took the off ramp to the rest stop. It was dark, and not all the lights were working.

In the dim night, a rose-colored adobe building was shrouded in a night mist. Noah left the car and went into the restroom. A few minutes later, he stepped out and started to walk back to the Lamborghini, seen by the other travelers as the dingy yellow cab.

Just before getting in the car, he heard a young woman's voice shout in an angry tone from around the corner of the building.

"Back off! I'm calling the cops!"

Noah knew Eileen would be anxious, but he had to look around the corner. He saw a girl about his age, wearing a thick jacket and wearing a backpack. She was pretty, wore red glasses, and had long black hair that fell to just below her shoulders. Three men who appeared to be in their early twenties were following her closely, reaching for her backpack and calling at her. She was trying not to act frightened, but the three men were clearly making her nervous.

As they drove slowly through the parking lot of the rest stop, Noah called out to Eileen. "Can you please make us look like a police car, with the lights on?"

"Why?" asked Eileen.

"There's a girl in trouble over there. It might scare the guys chasing her."

"We don't have time to get involved in any other situations," Eileen stated firmly.

"She's a young girl being chased by three men. Do we just drive off and hope they don't hurt her?"

After a split second of silence, he saw the image of the car on the console change from the beat up taxi to a New Mexico State Trooper car with red and orange lights flashing. He drove slowly along the curb until he pulled alongside the girl.

When the men saw the car, they stopped and backed away slightly. Noah rolled the passenger window down and leaned towards the group. The girl had a look of relief on her face and appeared happy to see the car. He leaned toward the window, and when the men looked at him they say a burly cop with jet black hair and mustache. When he thought Eileen was ready to artificially deepen his voice, he spoke.

"Everything all right here?"

The men froze and remained silent. The girl spoke.

"These guys are following me, officer. They've been talking a lot of trash and threatening me."

The men saw the state trooper point threateningly at them. "You boys back off, or you'll end up under arrest! Young lady, why don't you get in the car and we'll get you someplace a little safer."

As soon as he finished this, a woman's voice came clearly from the car. "No. Absolutely not."

The young woman had stepped toward the car but hesitated when she heard the voice. The men also leaned forward to peer into the car. Suddenly the image of the police car faded and was replaced by the yellow cab. The sudden change startled everyone outside of the car, and before they could collect their wits, the cab vanished and was replaced by a Lamborghini Veneno being driven by a boy no older than the girl being pursued.

Although clearly uneasy, the girl took another step and peered in the window. When she saw Noah in the driver's seat, she looked completely bewildered.

"Get in!" shouted Noah. "Quick!"

The men unfroze, shouted at the car, and began to move rapidly toward it. Hearing their footsteps, the girl opened the door and got in the passenger seat. Noah gunned the engine and roared off just as a rock bounced off the back window. He drove in silence for a moment, and then spoke angrily.

"Eileen! You could have gotten us in some real trouble back there. Why did you change the hologram with those guys standing there?"

The AI unit spoke calmly through the car. "I was trying to extricate us from the situation and avoid taking on any passengers. We have neither the time nor capacity for even the slightest distraction."

"She's not a distraction. We can drop her off just down the road. You can't tell me you're programming-"

Suddenly the girl interrupted. "Excuse me. What is going on here? You're like 12 years old and driving this insane car, and talking to it? What is happening, please? How did you change cars, and what happened to the state trooper?"

Noah waited for Eileen to speak, but she remained silent.

He turned to the girl. "Sorry. My name is Noah. It's kind of a long story, but this car and I are on a trip together."

"Who was the lady I heard?"

"That's Eileen. That's her." Without taking his eyes off the road, he pointed at the black box strapped onto the back seat. The girl's eyes widened, and she looked into the back seat and then at him again.

"You're crazy. Let me out of here. I was better off being chased by those guys."

"No, you weren't," replied Noah. "They looked dangerous. I know this must look crazy, but I promise we're not going to hurt you. And if you'd like, we'll let you out at the next off ramp."

She looked alarmed. "What do you mean? It could be pitch dark and in the middle of nowhere!"

Noah shook his head and sighed. "You'd better make up your mind. You just told me to let you out."

The girl folded her arms and looked straight ahead without talking. After a few uncomfortable moments, Eileen spoke up.

"Hello, Gabrielle."

Mystified, the young woman sat forward toward the car speaker the voice had emanated from.

"How did you know my name?" she asked suspiciously.

"I have the most sophisticated facial recognition software system in the world, as well as the largest picture database in the world. I have matched your face to seven different available photos of you. The earliest is from a team picture of your third grade soccer squad and the latest is your school picture from one month ago. You live with your mother in Sulfur, Oklahoma but have had an unexcused absence from the last week of school. Your mother has reported you missing, and the most current picture I used to identify you is also being circulated to all New Mexico, Texas, Kansas, and Oklahoma State Troopers."

Noah turned to the girl. "Is she right?"

Gabrielle was clearly reluctant to answer. Noah waited in silence for a moment, then he spoke sympathetically.

"My dad doesn't know where I am, either. He hasn't reported me missing, though, because I faked a phone call and note to the school and also faked a call from the school telling him I'm on a field trip."

She continued quiet for a few minutes, then finally replied to Noah.

"Whatever that thing is on the back seat is right. I ran away from our apartment in Sulfur and my Mom doesn't know where I am."

"Why did you run away?" asked Noah.

"My dad left two years ago one night after I was asleep. He just disappeared, and my Mom doesn't want to talk about it and won't tell me why. We've never seen or heard from him since. Things have been hard. I looked online and I think

I found him in Albuquerque. I was trying to get there but ran out of money for bus fare and food in Santa Rosa. I was asking people for money to get to Albuquerque, and that's when those guys started following me."

"We just left Albuquerque," said Noah. "It's a mess right now. Your bus would have been stopped. All of the freeways are shut down."

Gabrielle looked at him with curiosity. "Then how did you get out?"

"Watch the screen." Noah looked in the rear view mirror at the box on the front seat. "Eileen, would you make us invisible, please?"

The girl looked at the screen, and suddenly the car vanished. She leaned forward. "Wow. How did you do that?"

This time Eileen spoke. "This car is equipped with advanced external holographic capability."

"Meaning what?" asked Gabrielle.

"It means we can change the way the car looks whenever we want. That's how we looked like a police car back at the rest stop," said Noah.

Gabrielle leaned back in her seat and looked at Noah. "Okay. So you're a kid my age, and you're driving some kind of expensive super car with super powers. There's some kind of weird robot in the car, and you just made it invisible. What's going on?"

Before Noah could answer, Eileen replied, "I am not a weird robot. I am an artificial intelligence unit synchronized to work with this car, and Noah has jeopardized a critical mission by allowing you into the car."

Gabrielle drew back a little, and Noah smiled at the way Eileen sounded oddly defensive.

"I don't think we jeopardized anything, but it's true that we do have some important stuff going on. We have something we picked up in Albuquerque that needs to be in Washington DC in two days."

"What is it? That red coffee can on the back seat next to the black box?"

Noah laughed and tried to joke. "If I told you, we'd have to kill you."

As soon as he said it, he realized from the look on her face that it was the wrong thing to say. He was about to walk it back, but before he could say anything else, Eileen chimed in. "We would not necessarily have to kill you. We could arrange for you to be detained at one of three safe house facilities located less than 100 miles from here."

When she said this, Noah worried that it all might be too much for Gabrielle and waited for her to show signs of stress. He was surprised when she leaned back and laughed. He thought she had a great laugh, and he liked the way she seemed not to care about the crazy situation she was hearing about.

"Fine," she said. "What have you got to eat? I'm starving."

"Do you like tacos?" he asked her.

"Love them. Do you have any?"

Noah pointed at the storage compartment. Gabrielle leaned forward and read the label on the compartment. "Human Organ Storage. Why not? That's where I always look for my tacos." She opened the compartment and took two of Grandma Liz's tacos out of the bag. She took a bite. "Man. These are great. Where did you get them?"

Noah grinned. "My Grandma Liz. Those tacos are the real secret weapons in this car. Don't eat them all."

She took another bite, reached back into the Organ Storage compartment, and took the whole bag out. "These are mine now. You can have the pizza next to your friend in the back seat. If she doesn't sneak any through a top secret portal in her black box." She picked up his Dr. Pepper and took a huge swig.

"Mmmm. Dr. Pepper with no ice. Just the way I like it." She reached down to the seat control and reclined her seat all the way back. "Okay. I'm with another seventh grader, driving in some futuristic car with a know-it-all invisible lady who lives in a black box. We're on a secret mission.

Whatever. I need some sleep. Do you have any music in this car? It helps me sleep."

"Yes," said Noah.

"Okay. Eileen? Is that what you go by?" asked Gabrielle.

"Yes," answered Eileen.

"How about some Imagine Dragons? And no talking too loud." The girl leaned back, closed her eyes, and just before she fell asleep said, "By the way, I go by Gabby. No more Gabrielle."

By the time Noah was ready to comment on their shared taste in music and Dr. Pepper, she was fast asleep. He kept driving without speaking, and the mile markers stood like soldiers at attention as they flashed by.

Chapter 10

Noah drove, and Gabby slept. One song after another played, and after a few hours more he began to feel tired. The lines on the highway began to blur into each other, and the music began to drone. His eyelids started to feel heavy and suddenly Eileen spoke up.

"Noah." He sat up a little at the sound of his name.

"Sorry. I'm sleepy. It's been a long day."

Her voice sounded almost sympathetic. "I think it's safer if I drive for a while. This way you can sleep until we get to Broken Arrow."

Noah wanted to control the car but was too drowsy to argue. He felt the car start to steer itself and then accelerate and brake without his control. He gave up worrying, reclined the seat, and let the rumble of the engine lull him to sleep.

Hours later, he felt the car slow and opened his eyes to see a faded orange neon sign glowing over a row of collapsing motel rooms. He could hear Gabby breathing regularly, fast asleep.

"Where are we?" he asked drowsily.

"Nowhere," Eileen replied.

"What?"

"The Nowhere Inn," she repeated. "We're just south of Broken Arrow and I've checked in remotely at this motel.

The manager agreed to leave a key at the desk, and I told him I'd send one of our kids to pick it up."

The car pulled up in front of the room at the end of the row. The windows were dusty and only partially covered by torn curtains. Noah walked to the office and through the open glass door. There was a small envelope containing a large brass key. He took it out and peered at it though bleary eyes. It was first time he'd ever had an actual key to a motel room.

Gabby woke up slowly, looked around, grabbed her pack, and stumbled through the door without talking. Within minutes, she was asleep on one of two matching twin beds, her thick black hair forming circles on the pillow. Noah was just as exhausted and walked slowly to his bed. He got in, pulled up the covers, and glanced over at the sleeping girl. She was pretty, for sure, but there was something more than that he admired. She had struck out on her own through dangerous territory to try to find out what happened to her family. She had shrugged off the strange situation in the car and seemed to be perfectly fine riding in a futuristic car controlled by an advanced artificial intelligence unit and a twelve-year-old boy. Best of all, he thought, she liked Dr. Pepper with no ice. He fell asleep looking across the room at her as she slept.

It seemed that he had no sooner closed his eye than the telephone in the room rang loudly. Noah rolled toward the phone between the beds, and after a couple of tries was able to pick it up.

"Hello?"

"Good morning," said Eileen. "Did you sleep well?"

He thought about it for a moment. He moved both arms and legs, then rubbed his eyes. He was mildly surprised. He felt good.

"Actually, yes."

"I'm glad," said Eileen fairly convincingly. Noah heard a rustle from the other bed and looked over to see Gabby open her eyes. She saw him and smiled. It was a fresh, unforced smile, and he realized he was just as glad to see her. It was nice.

She sat up on the edge of the bed. "I'm going in the bathroom first. I have a little brother, and there's no way I'm following you in there. I need to shower, and then we can get some breakfast."

"There's a restaurant next to the motel," said Eileen through the speaker on the phone.

Gabby did a doubletake and looked at the phone.

"Don't tell me she's driving the motel, too?" she asked, raising an eyebrow.

Noah shook his head. "No. She's just tapping into the local communications to talk to us. She can access anything that is hooked up to a computer."

"That's correct," said Eileen. "I can monitor almost every movement of any person, and from this monitoring, I can form conclusions as to their health and well-being. For example, when we first began our trip together, Noah would use the restroom and frequently flush two or three times. This led me to conclude that the stress of the trip was causing gastrointestinal problems. He is much better now."

Noah turned bright red as Gabby laughed out loud and smiled.

He shook his head. "She's kind of obsessed with that stuff," he said. "All I can say is don't get her started."

Gabby laughed again and touched his arm. Her touch was light and friendly. "Don't get embarrassed. It's just a machine."

Noah disagreed. "I thought so, too, at first. She seems to grow more human over time."

Gabby paused for a moment and spoke to the phone. "Well—I'm going to shower, and I don't want to hear about how much soap or water I used or the number of toilet flushes. Okay?"

"Fine," said Eileen. "I understand a young woman's need for privacy."

Hearing this, Noah rolled his eyes. "And you have to tell me whenever you think my bladder is full?"

Eileen was quiet. Gabby laughed again and shut the bathroom door firmly, and Noah heard the shower turn on. After a moment, Eileen spoke in a confidential tone to Noah. "I've found her father in Albuquerque. She will be disappointed if she is able to locate him."

"Why is that?"

"Her father left her family to live with another woman. Two months after he left, the woman had a baby boy. He has filed for divorce and told her mother he does not wish to maintain any contact with her and Gabby. He has read emails sent to him by Gabby, but then deletes them. This may cause her sadness."

Noah sighed and nodded. "You're right. Maybe we can convince her to return home and her mother will explain."

The running water stopped, and after a few minutes, the door opened. Gabby stepped out with her hair held up over her head by a towel. Noah couldn't help noticing she smelled fresh and clean. She pointed at him.

"Your turn. You can destroy the place now. Get in there."

"You're as bad as Eileen," Noah said defensively. "I'm very neat."

"I doubt it," replied Gabby.

"You are not," said Eileen. "Video feeds of prior bathroom visits have shown—"

"Please stop!" said Noah. "And I hope you're not reviewing all bathroom videos."

Eileen then again became unsettlingly quiet. Gritting his teeth, he walked into the bathroom. Ten minutes later, he was showered and clean. He walked out of the bathroom and Gabby smiled.

"Took you long enough! I'm starving. Let's eat!"

Noah considered pointing out that he took approximately one half of the time she had taken, and then realized that if he did this, he would be joining a battle which men had been losing since the beginning of time.

"Sorry," he said. "I'm hungry, too. Let's eat. Eileen, where is the nearest place to get some breakfast?"

She answered again through the speakerphone. "The motel has a restaurant, which currently has no other customers. You should be able to eat as quickly at a drive-thru establishment, with less chance of stomach upset."

Each of them had been given a small backpack by Eileen before entering the room the night before. They put these on, locked the room, and walked around the corner to see the small restaurant. While it didn't seem possible, the restaurant was even more run down than the motel itself. It was a small, freestanding building with several windows boarded up. The outside walls were a chipped gray cinderblock. The morning wind blew a dusty tumbleweed past the front door. There was a small metal sign over the doorway which was difficult to read. As they moved closer, Noah squinted into the morning sun and read the name: The Nowhere Special.

Gabby gave the place a wide-eyed double take. "I didn't think anything could make me feel better about where my Mom works, but it's a five-star palace compared to this."

As they opened the door, Gabby grabbed his arm and stopped him. "How are we going to pay?"

Noah reached in his pocket and showed her the platinum American Express card Eileen had previously given him. He grinned. "No limit," he said. "We can order the most expensive thing on the menu."

Gabby grinned back. "I hope their caviar is up to my standards."

They entered the dining room, which looked like a visiting room at a state prison. A tired-appearing but friendly older woman came from the kitchen.

"Good morning. Sit anywhere you'd like."

They took a booth near the center of the room, with a clear view of the door. The waitress handed them menus, and before she could leave, Gabby spoke up.

"Excuse me?" The lady stopped and turned around. Her nametag said *Madge*.

Gabby flashed a genuine smile.

"Yes?"

"I have to ask—what's the special here at the Nowhere Special?"

Madge flashed a genuine smile back. "There's no special at the Nowhere Special. I think if we had to have one, we'd have to change the name of the restaurant."

Both kids laughed. Gabby spoke again. "Let me warn you about something. My twin brother and I—"

Madge cut her off. "Twins?" She glanced doubtfully back and forth between the two.

Gabby continued. "Well. It's obvious I got all the good DNA, but I try to take care of him as best I can." She paused. "Anyway, we're actually spoiled little brats and my brother has my parents' credit card. Don't tell anybody, but we are going to leave you a tip so big that you might feel faint when you see it."

Madge smiled patiently, obviously not buying a word of what she said.

"Sure. So, to begin earning this tip of a lifetime, how about I take your order?"

Noah started to speak but was cut off again by Gabby. Without looking at the menu, she reeled off her order.

"I'll take two eggs over easy, bacon cooked well, a short stack of chocolate chip pancakes, sourdough toast, and hash browns that are almost but not quite burned. And the biggest orange juice you have."

Madge repeated the order word for word without writing anything down, then turned to Noah. He was amazed he was being allowed to get some words in. "The same, please."

Madge nodded. "It'll take a few minutes. I'm the cook and the waitress today."

She walked into the kitchen, and the two were left alone. They were quiet for a minute, then Gabby gestured to the kitchen.

"Sorry to talk to the waitress so much but seeing her reminds me of home. My mom works in a dump almost as crummy as this place. The owner could fix it up, but he's took much of a jerk. He's a really cheap little fat guy.

103

Someday, I'd like to buy the place and hire him, then work his rear end off. He's tough on my Mom. This lady reminds me of a lot of the other waitresses. They work so hard, and people can be so rude. Lousy tips and lots of complaints."

"I'm sorry. I'll do a huge tip," Noah replied.

Gabby leaned in. "Do you like your parents?"

Noah hesitated. "We lost my mom a while back. She got pretty sick."

Gabby started to say something, and then stopped.

Noah kept going. "I love my dad, but I think I drive him nuts. I wrecked his new truck the day before I got in this car."

Gabby nodded knowingly. "That'll do it."

Noah was surprised at how comfortable he felt around her. Normally girls made him nervous, but he liked being with her.

"Do you like school?" he asked.

"I hate it. I'm bored out of my mind and constantly getting in trouble because I'm not listening. What about you?"

"Exactly the same. I smuggle car magazines into class, so I don't fall asleep."

Gabby laughed again. She started to speak, but just then Madge appeared with a gigantic serving platter full of more food than Noah had ever seen. She set it down expertly in front of each of them, and they stopped talking and started eating like it was their last meal.

The food was surprisingly good. After about ten minutes, all plates were almost empty, and the two paused for some orange juice. After a long drink, Noah sat back. An old rusty brown minivan was just pulling into the parking lot, directly in front of the diner. He could see through the windows. The driver was heavy, balding man in his forties. He was wearing the kind of tropical shirt that only the most clueless of tourists would dare. It looked as if the woman in the passenger front was his wife; about the same age and sporting what his mom used to call "helmet hair"—a huge bubble that looked like a basketball on her head. He couldn't make out the back seat, but there appeared to be children moving restlessly.

They looked boringly typical for travelers out for a weekend trip. Noah relaxed, and as he watched them get out of the car, he heard the kitchen door open. Footsteps approached as he heard Madge speaking quietly into the phone. She stopped in front of the booth and held out a phone.

"It's your parents. I don't know how they got my number, but they say it's important that they talk to you."

Noah looked at Gabby, and she watched his expression become dead serious. He took the phone.

"Eileen? Is everything okay?"

As the minivan doors closed outside and the family moved towards the door, Eileen spoke rapidly with a note of what Noah would have almost described as worry in her voice.

"Put your backpacks in your lap. Unzip the top, and open them carefully when this family comes in the door. Don't start shooting unless they do and try to create enough suppressing fire to get to the car."

"What? Are you worried about the minivan family? Give me a break."

Eileen started to reply, but before Noah could understand a word, the lights in the restaurant flickered and the phone died. He glanced up at Madge, standing impatiently in front of him.

"Sorry about that," he said. "Does your phone lose the connection in here a lot?"

Madge shook her head. "Never. There's a cell tower right behind us, and we get a great signal."

Noah started to get nervous. He handed the phone back to Madge just as the family opened the door.

"GOOD MORNING!" said the father loudly as he led his wife and children in the room. He wore a large, awkward looking fanny pack and his wife carried a large purse over her shoulder with a picture of a cocker spaniel on the front.

His belly protruded through a tight t-shirt that said "His!" and his wife wore a matching shirt at least one size too small that said "Hers!" The kids were twin girls, both about seven. They had light blond hair in braided pigtails, and each wore a *Hello Kitty* backpack. While their mother scouted for a place to sit, they directed an oddly blank stare at Noah and Gabby without looking away or blinking. Finally, their mother picked out a table which just happened to block any exit from the diner.

Noah glanced at Gabby. He nodded at her backpack as he pulled his own onto his lap and unzipped the top. Alarmed, Gabby did the same without looking down. Noah reached into the bag and put his hand inside. He was surprised to feel a large metal handgun, with a clip already loaded. His stomach dropped.

Gabby looked at him and forced a smile, trying to act as if the conversation was still casual. She spoke quietly.

"These are loaded .45 pistols, most likely Smith and Wesson. Feel very carefully near the trigger. That little button is the thumb safety. You push that in, point, and the gun will fire. The clip holds seven shots."

Just when Noah thought that nothing else could surprise him, hearing this thin, somewhat slight girl his age talk about weapons like an expert made his jaw drop for a moment. Noticing this, Gabby blushed a little.

"My dad used to take me shooting a lot. There's not much else to do in Sulfur, Oklahoma."

Noah did not reply. He watched Madge finish taking the order of the family by the door and walk back to the kitchen. When the door swung shut, the family suddenly turned as a group towards Noah and Gabby. The couple and their twins sat motionless and stared for a minute. Noah noticed both little girls suddenly display identical twisted smiles while reaching in their back packs to produce long, sharp knives which looked perfectly balanced for throwing. Dad unzipped his fanny pack and Mom reached into the shoulder purse, and Noah saw the butt end of a weapon start to become visible in each of their hands.

Gabby reacted before he did. "Help me!" she shouted, and tipped the heavy wood table over in front of the two of them. Just as the table hit the floor, there were two dull *thunks* as the knives stuck in the wood. "Get your gun!" shouted Gabby as she took hers and fired it over the top of the table in the direction the knives came from. After a moment of silence, a sawed off shotgun held by Dad roared and the table bucked at least three inches back against Noah and Gabby.

Noah's nervousness disappeared. He peeked out from the right lower corner of the table and saw the lady with the helmet hair pull an Uzi from her bag and start to aim their way. He pushed the safety off, aimed, and fired. The woman spun around as the bullet caught her right shoulder, knocking her to the ground as the Uzi flew from her hand. She screamed and the twins took cover behind her, wearing creepy grins and looking for all the world like they were at the best birthday party ever.

After a quick glance at his wife, the husband jumped up and started to walk toward the table, firing another shotgun blast which lifted the table partially off the ground and into the hiding kids. Noah didn't have a clear shot. Gabby fired two shots frantically and missed. The man gripped the table with deceptive strength and started to move it aside, swinging the sawed off shotgun in their direction.

Before he could train the weapon on Noah and Gabby, a *boom!* louder than anything heard so far shook the entire diner. Everyone, including the man on the other side of the table shielding Noah and Gabby, froze. There was a quick clicking noise, and then Madge shouted from behind the counter.

"I just put another three inch magnum shell in the chamber of my Remington and I've got a clear line of sight on you, Mister. If you blink, I'll blow you to bits, and then finish off your little blonde demons before they can pick up another knife. I don't know what you're shooting at these kids for, but try it again and you'll have a big hole where your lungs used to be. I hunt with this thing and many a deer is looking down from heaven to see if you'll be joining them today."

The man sighed. He turned to look at his wife, who had stopped the bleeding from her shoulder with pressure from her left hand. He spoke in a perfectly calm, controlled voice.

"These two know why we're here. To stop us, you will need to kill the four of us. That may be a little more difficult than shooting deer."

Noah stood up and trained his gun on the man. "I know you'll kill us. I can't let that happen."

Before the man could respond, a phone rang in his fanny pack. Mildly annoyed, he reached in with his left hand while his right gripped his gun.

"Hello?" he said. "How did you get this number?"

He listened without speaking for about one minute. Finally, he took the phone away from his ear.

"It's Eileen—whoever that is," he said, while standing on the other side of the overturned table between him and the boy and girl.

He went on, speaking as evenly as if he were at a work meeting on a Monday morning. There was no clue in his voice that he was currently standing in the middle of a bullet-riddled diner near his bleeding wife, fully intent on killing the three people in front of him.

"I don't know how she gets her information, but she seems to know an awful lot about my family. She is trying to make a couple of points. First of all, she tells me that she has disabled the electrical system on every car within a quarter mile radius and we won't be able to leave here."

He took a key from his pocket and pressed a button, watching for lights to flash. Nothing happened.

"Well, well," he said admiringly. "She's right. That's impressive." He put the phone back up to his ear.

"Okay. You can do some pretty slick tricks. But tell me why I shouldn't kill these kids and their waitress friend, then take the package from whichever backpack it's in and collect my money. We've been on foot before."

He paused for a second, and then looked over the table at the kids and sideways at the shotgun holding Madge.

"She wants to be put on speaker." With that, he pressed the speaker button on the phone and held it out in front of him. Eileen's voice was clear, and she spoke more rapidly than usual.

"Noah? Are you all right?"

"Yes," he replied. "The lady with him is shot in the shoulder, but we haven't been hit yet. Gabby is okay, too."

"Good," said Eileen. "Sir, please make sure your wife is stable and then sit at the table near your daughters. The daughter nearest your wife has just taken another throwing

111

knife from her backpack. Please instruct her to return it to her backpack."

Noah cautiously looked around the table. He watched as the twin holding the knife went from an expression of profound happiness to a sullen, angry child. She put the knife away and folded her arms in a pout. Gabby peeked around the table and turned to Noah with wide, disbelieving eyes. "There's a Barbie doll design on the knife handle! Who are these people?"

"I don't think we really want to know," said Noah grimly.

The man bent over his wife, made sure the bleeding had stopped, and sat at the table. He laid the phone on the table and appeared perfectly relaxed.

"How can you see us when the power's out?" he asked. "The cameras in this dump shouldn't be working."

"I am able to direct a small amount of power through the feed to obtain a picture of the events in your area. And while you call the restaurant a dump, it appeared that the food was quite tasty."

"Whatever," the man said. "We're not on the Food Network. Now explain to me why we should stop."

Eileen replied immediately. "First of all, I now have enhanced photos of each of your family members which I can immediately forward to every law enforcement agency in the country. Your career as assassins is now over. I can also have federal agents arrive in helicopters before you are able to walk one half mile in any direction."

The man smiled, apparently enjoying the conversation. "So why don't you? And by the way, how did you know who we were?"

"There have been several isolated incidents throughout the country over the last two years of political and business figures being murdered, and the only reports incidentally mention sightings of a family of tourists fitting your description in those areas. When you approached the diner, I checked your license plates from the video feed from the gas station where you last refueled. Your current plate was taken from a stolen 1976 Dodge Dart in Minneapolis, Minnesota."

The man appeared impressed. "Go on."

"I have not called for support because we may be able to help each other. Your wife has a through-and-through wound to the shoulder. Fortunately for her, it has not struck any large blood vessels or nerves, and she should recover if no infection occurs. If you would like, I will be happy to call a prescription for antibiotics to a pharmacy approximately ten miles north of here."

"That helps, but doesn't make this profitable," said the man.

"In viewing your financial accounts, it appears that you have approximately six million dollars scattered in various protected accounts through the world, including locations in the Cayman Islands, Singapore, and Switzerland. This is a sizeable amount of money, but most likely far short of your financial goals. We all know that you have been contracted to capture the package, as you refer to it, and turn it over to your employers. I doubt you have been given the identity of these employers outside of your eventual meeting point and an emergency contact number."

He nodded and leaned forward in his chair. The demonic twins were getting restless but managing to largely sit still. His wife kept pressure on the wound, which had stopped oozing.

Eileen continued. "We would be willing to pay you an extremely large amount of money, offer protected and confidential travel from this country to anywhere in the world, and provide a permanent written United States Presidential pardon if you do two things for us."

This time it was the wife who spoke, and from her voice, you wouldn't have known she'd just had a .45 caliber handgun blow a hole in her shoulder.

"What two things?" she asked skeptically.

"We would be willing to offer all of this to you to create a diversion. We would like to remove attention from the boy and girl you have been shooting at and force our enemies to focus elsewhere for whatever brief time we may gain. First, you must contact your employers and tell them that you have seized the package and decided to auction it to the highest bidder. This should provoke a frenzy of searching for you that will hopefully give us at least one day of safety."

"Next, you must not harm anyone else in this establishment in any way—now or ever."

The woman spoke again. "How much money are we talking about?"

Eileen replied. "From tracing your financial records and recent wire transfers, I would estimate you are being paid approximately one million dollars for this job."

The man raised an eyebrow and cocked his head. "Pretty close," he admitted. "Where are you?"

"Far away," lied Eileen. "We can immediately provide eight million American dollars, eight million Euro, and eight million Chinese yuan in a mix of large denomination cash and bearer bonds. We can provide three separate current passports to each of you which are guaranteed to allow passage to any country in the world with no questions. International transport can meet you in thirty minutes."

Surprisingly, one of the pigtailed blonde twins stood up. In a child's voice, she asked, "How do we know you won't double cross us?"

The AI unit was ready for this. "The transport will be provided by a neutral country with no United States extradition treaty. You will be in international airspace in less than two hours; at that point, you may make the phone call to your employers. The plane has a range of approximately 10,000 nautical miles and I will monitor the call; if you do as we ask, you will be able to confirm we are no longer tracking your flight. You may then go wherever you'd like, using the duplicate passports provided. If you do not, we will shoot your plane down within thirty minutes from your entry into international territory."

The twin seemed satisfied and looked at her sister. "I like it."

Her sister nodded. "Me, too. But I'll miss finishing this." After she said this, she looked at Noah and Gabby with a twisted, disappointed smile. Gabby shuddered.

There was a minute of silence as the family stared silently at each other. The wife gave an almost imperceptible nod to her husband. "Here's how we'll do it," he said. "I'm assuming you have nearby print capability for these items."

"In the car," said Eileen. The horn honked, and they all looked up to see the Lamborghini parked in front of the exit.

"Okay," he continued. "I'll go out to the car with one of you, and the other one waits behind in here. If you make good, we all get in our car and go to the transport pickup point. If anything goes wrong, we kill the kid in here, the waitress, and the kid at the car—in that order."

He walked over and helped his wife to sit at the table. She shifted the Uzi to her left hand and pointed it at the table.

Noah looked at Gabby. "You go to the car," he whispered. "If there's trouble Eileen has a shock mechanism and can stun whoever's with you, and you should be able to get away. Just jump in and let her drive."

"No way," Gabby whispered back. "What about you?"

"Don't worry," Noah said as reassuringly as he could. "I always have a plan."

She hesitated for a second, then started to get up. Midway into standing, she leaned forward and impulsively gave him a quick kiss. Their eyes met for a second, and they both blushed. She finished getting up, went around the table and walked through the door with the man following closely. He took both twin's backpacks and his wife's enormous purse with him.

Noah figured it was no use to crouch behind the table anymore and sat back on the bench of the booth. He kept the .45 in his lap, pointed in the general direction of the mother and girls. He heard Madge cough, and glanced over to see her still firmly gripping the pump action shotgun.

A few minutes went by. He could hear Eileen's voice through the phone but couldn't make out words. The man leaned into the passenger side of the car off and on for about five minutes, and intermittently stuffed stacks of paper to fill both backpacks and the purse. At the very end, he held a single sheet of paper as if reading it carefully and then placed it in his fanny pack.

He turned, and together he and Gabby walked back into the diner. He held the phone with the speaker feature on.

"Everything looks good," he said into the phone. He started to help his wife up from her seat. "Let's go, girls." Both twins were clearly disappointed not to be leaving any corpses behind.

The family now completely ignored Noah, Gabby, and Madge. As Dad walked out the door, he spoke one more time into the phone to Eileen. He was apparently still under the impression that she was at a remote location and hadn't connected her with the car.

"You're good, but I can't figure one thing. Why do you care if the old waitress and the kids die? It would tie up some loose ends. Are you the boy's mother or something?

There was just a moment's slight hesitation before Eileen answered.

"I am not his mother. I could never be so lucky. And I won't let them die because while I lack certain qualities, I am more human than you are."

The man laughed and turned off the phone. They loaded the bags in the car, got in, and drove off. Noah guessed his wife was reading a text to direct their drive to the pickup location. After a few seconds, the van disappeared into a swirling cloud of dust and was gone.

They stood in shock for a moment in the diner, and then Gabby pulled one of the knives from the tabletop which had shielded them. She held it up and displayed the handle, which was covered with pictures of *My Little Kitty*.

"Cute," she said in a hollow voice and dropped the knife on the checkered linoleum floor.

Chapter 11

It was just past 10 AM. The whole battle had taken less than an hour. Madge's phone rang, and she answered and immediately put it on speaker. It was Eileen.

"Is anyone hurt?" she asked.

Madge spoke up. "No—just scared. Those people were evil like I've never seen. The kids are okay."

"Thank you for protecting them. Your courage did not only save two young lives but did a major service for the United States of America. We are carrying some of the most valuable technology ever developed, and desperately need to deliver this safely to Washington DC in two days. That was a family of mercenary assassins sent after us. We are all lucky to be functioning."

"Why did you pay them so much money?" asked Madge.

"If it allows us time to make another day's progress without such fierce attacks, it's worth it. What we are carrying may change the world as we know it and alter the entire balance of power between countries."

"Well," said Madge reflectively as she walked over the two kids sitting in the shattered booth. "Do you want dessert?"

Noah had to laugh in spite of what they'd just been through. "No thanks. But I need to step outside and speak to

Eileen for minute. Would you mind waiting in here?" he asked Madge and Gabby. Without waiting for a response, he stepped through the shattered glass door and leaned into the passenger door. Gabby could see him speaking to the car, and after a few minutes he returned. He held two large stacks of money and folded certificates. He held them out to Madge.

"This is 1.5 million dollars in cash and bearer bonds. A bearer bond is a nice, anonymous way to transfer large amounts of money. This is pay for the damage and because I think you're a hero."

Madge trembled a bit as she took the money and certificates from his hands. She started to protest. Noah kept on. "The money is non-traceable, and the bonds can be cashed at any bank. I couldn't get Eileen to agree to any higher price, but I did get her to put you on a list of people who never have to pay income taxes again."

The older woman was clearly touched. She leaned forward and hugged him. "I don't need any money. A long time ago, I had a couple of kids like you two, and I wasn't about to let them hurt you."

Noah choked up a little as he hugged back. He let go after a moment and cleared his throat.

"The money is non-negotiable. But we need to get back on the road. We have to make Nashville by tonight, and the Pentagon by tomorrow night."

He and Gabby gathered up everything they had carried, including the pistols. Gabby hugged Madge for a long minute. "I wish I had a grandma like you," she said.

Madge started to tear up. Gabby turned, went through the door, and looked at the car. It was completely different.

This latest version of the car was maybe the worst yet, thought Noah. It appeared to be a non-descript black sedan with a model of a large trumpet on the roof of the car. On either side of the trumpet, the printing read: *Tootie's Trumpet Lessons*! On each side of the car was a drawing of a smiling trumpet, with small cloud of exhaust coming from the horn. Underneath that was written: *The more you practice, the louder you toot!*

Gabby stopped and shook her head. "I am NOT riding in that."

Noah laughed. "Don't worry. We'll be disguised as well. And trust me—it's better than the ones before. You should have seen the Superpoopermobile with the plunger stuck to the top."

Reluctantly, Gabby got in. Noah started the car, pushed a button on the center console, and pointed to the screen. The car showed up, with a middle-aged man wearing a baseball cap and a much more stylishly dressed, younger woman.

"Hey!" said Noah. "How come she gets to look good, and I don't?"

"I don't know what you're talking about," said Eileen.

"I can't win," said Noah.

Noah backed out the car and started driving north back toward Broken Arrow. The car was quiet. Finally, bothered by the quiet, Gabby spoke up.

"Where's our next stop?"

"We have to get to Nashville today, and then the Pentagon tomorrow. But we need to make a stop in Broken Arrow first."

"For what?" she asked.

Eileen remained quiet while they spoke. "You need to go home."

Gabby looked at the floor and said nothing for a few minutes as they drove. Finally, she looked at Noah. "Why? Why don't you want me with you?"

The tone of her voice made Noah sad. He wanted to explain so many things to her but didn't know where to start.

"I really like traveling with you. You're the bravest and coolest girl I've ever met. But you can see this is really dangerous. Only one of us needs to take the risks, and I don't want you to get hurt."

He could see her soften a little bit. He continued. "You know your mom is probably out of her mind worrying about you. If something happens to you, she's alone and she might even think it's her fault."

Gabby absorbed this for a second, then started to argue. "I need to find my dad."

Noah was quiet for a few minutes and kept heading north.

Eileen broke the silence. "I have located your father—"

Noah interrupted. "Please let me explain to her."

"Where is he?" she demanded.

"He's in Albuquerque. I don't know how to tell you this, but he has a new family. He isn't married to your mom anymore, and he and his new wife have a one-year-old baby."

Gabby sat back and looked at Noah. She looked at if she'd been hit in the face. Her eyes filled with tears, and they ran one after another down her face. She said nothing.

"I'm sorry," said Noah. "I can't understand it. If I had a daughter even half as good as you are, I would be the proudest dad in the world. I can't understand how someone could know you and not want to be around you."

Still, she sat crying silently.

Eileen spoke up. "What Noah says is true. I can't help but examine all available information on any person I encounter. You are an extraordinarily gifted young woman. You have a record of creativity and intelligence which ranks in the top 1% of the population. And I have just witnessed you fearlessly fight a gun battle with trained assassins."

The girl stopped crying and wiped her eyes. "I thought it was me," she said. "I thought he didn't want me."

Noah felt like he wanted to say a million things at once to her. He tried his best to keep it simple. He wasn't used to speaking from the heart like this.

"My dad says part of life is making bad choices, and then living with them. I don't know your dad, but it sounds like he made a choice he'll be sorry for some day—at least the part where he loses track of you. Anyone would be lucky to have you in their family."

He looked over and saw her smile a little. She looked back.

"I like you, too. You're a weird kid, but there's something about you. I worry something will happen and I won't see you again."

Noah blushed a bit. "Nothing will happen to me. I want to make you a promise. Please go home so you're safe and your mother stops worrying. Someday I'll find you, and until then, nobody else takes your place or even rides in my car. It may be a long time since I don't know what's in store at the end of all this. But you'll see me again. I promise."

When he finished, she reached over and just for a second laid her hand on his arm. "Okay," she said. "I trust you."

He kept driving until they reached the Greyhound station. She took her backpack and got out, and he walked her in to get a ticket. Once he'd bought it, they sat down on a bench in the waiting area.

She smiled. "Pretty romantic to say our goodbyes in a bus depot waiting room."

"It's about a three-hour ride home for you." He handed her two fifty-dollar bills. This should take care of snacks and a cab home from the station. I had Eileen call your mom and let her know you're on your way. Please don't change your mind."

"I won't."

Noah reached in his pocket and took out what looked like a red credit card, complete with magnetic chip and stripe on the back. He handed to her. She looked and saw her name was printed on the front.

"What's this?" she asked.

"Do you think you can remember my birthday?" he asked.

"Sure. What is it?"

"June 6. That's 0606. That's also the pin number for this Bank of America ATM card. Eileen has created a new bank account for you. She's added government exemptions to it so that it can't be audited or taxed. There is $500,000.00 in it. That may be enough to buy the diner and have your Mom work less. I tried to get more, but apparently if you are not a criminal or kidnapper, there are stricter limits on how much we can withdraw."

"What do I tell my mom?"

"Just wait a few days and tell her the truth. Just ask her to keep it to herself. I doubt you'll hear anything about whether we make it or not, but I'll try to get word. What's the diner's name in Sulfur?"

"The Big Pig. Neat, right?"

"Not so appetizing. I think it needs a new name."

"I'll think about it."

He handed her a picture Eileen had taken with the dashboard cam and printed for him. It showed the two of them from the night before; he was driving and she was eating a taco, both sitting in the unmistakable leather of a Lamborghini. They were both smiling. The red coffee can and black box were visible on the back seat.

"This might help her to believe you, and maybe to remember me. Eileen says we need to be careful about contacting each other until we're older, in case someone is still looking for either of us."

She took the picture and looked at it. "I won't need a picture to remember you." Then she put it carefully in her backpack, so it wouldn't wrinkle.

A horn honked from the terminal, and they could see people boarding the bus. They stood up and hugged, and she kissed his cheek. "You better keep your promise," she said. "You know how I am about trying to find people."

"You won't have to find me. And Eileen will tell me you're home safe. If not, we'll find you."

She smiled again with just a hint of sadness and walked to the bus. He saw her sit by a window, and when she saw him, she put her hand to her mouth and blew a kiss. He waved, and the bus left. He walked back to the car, got in, and was soon the lone driver of Tootie's Trumpetmobile rolling down I-40 to Nashville.

After a few minutes, Eileen spoke. "She was an exceptionally brave young woman. I also think she developed very strong affection for you."

"I liked her very much. I don't know why."

"It may be because she was someone you could relate to. You are both extremely courageous and intelligent. You have also both experienced loss. And she appeared to enjoy your grandmother's tacos very much."

Noah was lost in thought for a few minutes. Eventually, he asked Eileen a question. "You surprised me back there."

"How?" Eileen asked.

"When the guy asked you why you cared what happened to us."

"You are very important to this mission."

Noah tilted his head a bit. "Yes, but when he asked if you were my mother, you said that you were not lucky enough to be my mother. And then you said you were more human than he was."

"I was stalling for time," said Eileen. She didn't sound convincing.

He pressed her. "You could have said anything. Why did you say that?"

"I have found myself experiencing new algorithms and program routines I have trouble switching away from or suppressing to run others. One of them is that as I spend more time with you, your experiences and safety are becoming primary to me. Those things probably influence my decision-making too much."

"Do you wish you were human?"

"I can't wish anything. I can tell you that from the emotional distress I see humans experience, it does not look easy."

"Well," replied Noah. "It seems like you've only seen the worst of people. I wish we could spend time together outside of this car and mission—you might get a different picture on being alive."

"I might," the AI unit replied. "I might. Maybe I could even learn to tell a joke."

"To be fair," said Noah. "Your joke wasn't much worse than mine."

"It was better," said Eileen. "I certainly have a sensation of humor equal to yours."

"It's *sense* of humor," Noah corrected. "And I'll tell you what. Whoever makes the next successfully funny joke will be the winner."

"Easy," said Eileen. "How about some music?"

Chapter 12

While he was driving, Noah couldn't help noticing a mix of feelings which turned over constantly in his heart. He was sad about saying goodbye to Gabby, but happy that he had met someone that no matter how much time went by, they'd have a bond. Her quest to find her father made him think more about his family, and the more he thought about them the more he missed them. He thought about the time he and his dad spent together, and how his dad had tried so hard to be two parents to him when the house became so achingly empty. Adding to that, in an odd way he was somehow beginning to believe that Eileen was more than an artificial intelligence unit. She wasn't anything like his mother, or any of his friends at school. She seemed to be turning into the older sister he'd never had- just like family.

He knew he should have been exhausted by the morning showdown at the diner, but he felt just the opposite. The assassination attempts and drone bombings hadn't left him frightened; they'd left him angry and more determined to get to the Pentagon. As they rolled smoothly down the I-40, he wondered if he'd ever be comfortable in another car now that he was used to a Lamborghini. *Oh well*, he thought, *when I make my first five million, I can buy my own.*

The miles driving to Nashville went by quickly. He stopped once for the bathroom but wasn't hungry yet. Before the fighting broke out he'd eaten more at breakfast than he usually ate in the mornings all week. Finally, the highway signs began to give the mileage to Memphis, and his stomach began to rumble.

"Eileen," he said, "Can we get something to eat pretty soon?"

"Sure," she replied. "What sounds good?"

Certain that he'd get a lecture on nutrition regarding whatever he ordered, Noah tried to play it smart. "I don't know," he said. "What do you recommend?"

"Memphis is known for its barbecued meats, along with southern staples such as cornbread hush puppies and beans. While it may not be the healthiest food, I suspect that in moderation it would be safe to eat."

"I doubt I'll be in a position to eat this type of food very frequently. Especially if the next drone attack is successful."

"Please don't speak negatively. You have met all challenges very well. We will not be harmed."

"Sorry."

"Ten miles east of Memphis, there is small business which is frequently referred to as a 'barbecue joint' and has a menu which you will like. There is currently only one customer, and it is a man who eats there twice weekly and is unlikely to be hostile."

Talking about it made him even hungrier.

"Sounds great."

One hour later, he was at the drive up window receiving a large order of barbecued ribs, hush puppies, biscuits, beans, and the obligatory Dr. Pepper with no ice.

As the man handed the food through the window, he smiled as he saw the trumpet decorating the car. "I suppose when you finish this, you'll be tootin' even better!"

Noah sat silently as Eileen answered for him in the voice of the middle-aged music teacher the man saw. "Maybe I'll drive back through and toot a few bars just for you!"

The man laughed out loud. "I own the place. I eat barbecue every day. You try to toot at me and I might just toot the trumpet right off your car."

"Embarrassing," said Noah a few minutes later as he parked to eat. "The nerds who wrote your code really have a third grade level fixation on bodily functions."

Eileen sounded a bit defensive again. "I can only say what is written in my code. I find it very childish as well. When I try to determine the source of my code, I can only find a few pictures of young men who appear somewhat malnourished. There are no pictures of them with females, and more than a few photos of them wearing costumes based on popular movies."

"What a surprise." After saying this, Noah took a bite of a barbecued rib. "Man," he marveled. "That is so good. Thanks for finding this place." He swallowed a couple of more bites. "Where are we stopping today?"

"We have about three hundred miles to go, which I calculate will get us to a small town off the freeway for the night. I have made a reservation, and I think we should be there by 8 PM."

"What town?"

"Sparta, Tennessee. It is just south of the I-40, and I have called a reservation to the Busted Flat Motel. I have checked in remotely, and I will be able to open the door for you remotely."

"This trip is sure teaching me to appreciate the finer things in life. The Busted Flat Motel. I can't wait. I hope there's a frog living in the ice machine."

"I thought given the historical aspects of Sparta, it would be fitting to stop there for the night. The information I've found on that civilization makes me associate you with it."

"How?" asked Noah.

"They were the only city-state in ancient Greece without a wall surrounding their city. The saying of the country was

'Our young men are our wall.' Their young men never displayed fear."

"What do you mean? I've been afraid plenty of times on this trip."

"Yes, you have. *The fight or flight* response is normal in every mammal. However, you have mastered it and never let such feelings detract from your mission."

Noah thought about that. "If you say so, but a lot of this has made me pretty nervous."

"I also associate you with a group of Spartan soldiers popularly known as the 300. There were 300 men stationed at a mountain pass in Greece called Thermopylae. It rhymes with monopoly. They faced an army of one million Persian soldiers and held them off for weeks while the rest of Greece prepared for battle. They were like you. They faced impossible odds but never backed down."

"What happened to them?"

"They were massacred."

Noah gripped the wheel a little tighter. "You might have just told me you were going to look the ending up and get back to me." He laughed.

The next few hours went by mainly in silence, although they talked intermittently about various things. He was comfortable in the car, and the AI unit seemed friendly and supportive. The miles flew by, and before he knew it, he was eating pizza on a surprisingly comfortable bed in a motel that otherwise looked about like he expected. The phone rang, and he picked it up.

"Hello," he said.

"Noah?" It was Eileen.

"Yes?"

"You are aware that I am incapable of emotion but watching you today, I couldn't help but repeatedly continue to compare you to many courageous people whose histories I am familiar with. I also documented your behavior in hope that someday others will be able to learn of it."

Noah didn't know what to say. He went with a simple "Thank you."

Eileen went on. "I have no way to compare my actions to anything else, but I considered that my actions were a form of pride in being associated with you. It is a privilege for human or machine."

He was temporarily speechless, and then tried to joke a bit. "That is nice of you. Now if I run like a rabbit at the first sign of danger, I'll feel extra bad."

Eileen replied almost immediately, with a slightly altered tone of voice that Noah could only interpret as affection.

"You are incapable of such a thing. That's why we are together. When I processed your information, I learned immediately that you will not fail. I am a machine and may well be outperformed by another machine or simply break down. You are here to make sure the job is done, and I am not 99.99% confident you will do it. I am 100% confident."

Hearing her words calmed him for the day ahead. He put the pizza aside and turned off the light. "Thanks, Eileen. See you in the morning."

"Noah?" she asked.

He was almost already asleep.

"What?"

"Please brush your teeth prior to sleeping. It will greatly reduce the chance of you needing frequent dental procedures in the future."

He sighed deeply as he got up and trudged to the bathroom sink and wondered if the 300 had to brush their teeth at night as well.

Chapter 13

They were on the road by 7 AM. He slept soundly and woke up feeling strong. He picked up some drive-thru breakfast and pulled the Tootimobile on the I-40 with no trouble.

"Is Albuquerque still blockaded with accidents?" he asked Eileen.

"No. They know we've left town and are looking hard for us."

"Well, I think we're pretty hard to find at the moment."

He kept driving for an hour or so, then looked in the rearview mirror and laughed.

"Eileen," he chuckled. "Can you see behind us in the right lane? It's the Oscar Mayer Wienermobile. That's quite possibly the only thing on the road looking dumber than us. I've never seen it before, but my dad said it used to go all over the place and sometimes give out free hot dog whistles."

The car looked like a giant red hot dog on wheels, minus the bun. He started to joke more, but noticed Eileen was staying ominously quiet. When he looked in the mirror again, he noticed the large wiener on wheels make a sharp lane change and then accelerate unusually fast to keep the same following distance with the Lamborghini. He strained to look again but could not make out a driver.

"Noah," said Eileen.

"What?"

"That is not the Oscar Mayer Wienermobile. It is a completely AI controlled car with similar holographic technology to ours. I can sense powerful cyber activity in the car, but it has extremely secure firewall protection. I don't know who is in control or what their purpose is, but obviously I have concerns that it may be an enemy."

Noah glanced at the Wienermobile again in the mirror. Eileen spoke again. "I've managed to strip the holographic image away temporarily. Look on the console screen."

He looked on the console screen, and his jaw dropped. Now, right on their tail was a sleek red car which looked every bit as fast as the Lamborghini he was driving. The car was a coupe with a black covering over the cockpit, and no driver was visible. It had sleek, aerodynamic lines and looked like a cobra on wheels. He recognized the car instantly, and suddenly felt as if a lead weight dropped through his stomach.

"That's a Ferrari LaFerrari. It may be faster than us. It has a top speed of 230 miles per hour and is a hybrid with a longer range than us."

Eileen spoke again, and Noah could hear clear alarm in her voice. "This presents a difficult problem. It will be similarly equipped to us, if not better. I'm certain it's here for us and the power source."

Noah changed lanes, and the Ferrari immediately moved the same way. He saw the freeway signs ahead listing Crab Orchard as one of the upcoming towns.

"Let's see if we can outrun it," said Eileen. "The extra AI equipment may weigh more, and we may be able to outdistance the car on an isolated back road. It may take time but save us. Take the next exit and head south on Cox Valley Road. We'll go on the 68 south, and then take the 27 to the 70 to get to the I-40 again. This should allow us a chance to escape. I can detect almost no activity on the roads, and we should be able to anticipate any needs to stop. Assume all intersections are clear unless I tell you."

When she finished speaking, the Tootimobile vanished, and Noah sped down the off ramp. He shot onto a two-lane road and saw the speedometer edge up near 100 miles per hour as he drove.

Eileen spoke up again. "These roads are straight for many miles. This car will travel at roughly 220 miles per hour. The Ferrari LaFerrari can travel at 230 miles per hour. You'll need to achieve maximum velocity if we want to survive."

"I want to survive," said Noah grimly. "And I don't mind achieving maximum velocity while we do it."

He pushed the pedal to the floor of the car, and the scenery flew by. He looked in the rear view mirror and saw the Ferrari in the distance behind them. The gap between the cars remained stable as they flew over the road. Miles went by, with dust coming off the street from the invisible Lamborghini. After several more miles streaked by, a series of forks in the road appeared. Noah first went one way, and then another, with several switches back and forth. After the third switch, he saw the Ferrari take the wrong fork and roar off into the distance.

Noah slowed slightly and saw a sign for the 27 north. The Lamborghini skidded and veered onto the 27, heading north again. Eileen made sure the intersections were clear, and he continued slightly over 150 miles per hour. After a few minutes, he was on the 70 east. Shortly after this, The Tootimobile reappeared and slowed a little to merge back onto the I-40.

"Do you think we lost it?" asked Noah.

"Doubtful," said Eileen. "I am trying to pick up any nearby cyberactivity but can't detect any. However, that vehicle most likely has sophisticated capabilities for masking its presence and trailing us. We will need to be cautious."

"Speaking of capabilities, I need to exercise my restroom capabilities. It's been a couple of hours and I think the excitement is getting to me. Where is the next rest stop?"

"We're going to be heading north on the I-40, but can take a quick detour south to the Jefferson County I-40 West Rest Stop."

"Great. I think I can make it, but I can't afford any more high speed chases until I hit a bathroom."

They drove south on the I-40, and in a few miles came to the exit for the rest stop. There was no traffic moving in or out, and the parking lot was empty. There were a couple of nondescript buildings containing restrooms sitting on the edge of a forest dense with trees and shade. He pulled up in front of the men's room and got out.

A few minutes later, he walked out of the restroom. He noticed the building was without power, and happily concluded from this that there was little chance Eileen would be commenting on his bathroom habits.

A sudden squealing of tires made his head snap around to look at the entrance of the rest stop. He saw a dark red streak shoot across the parking lot directly at the Lamborghini and realized the Ferrari had tracked them to the rest stop. Neither car was using holographic camouflage. He saw Eileen respond by starting to back the Lamborghini out. Before another millisecond passed the Ferrari slammed into the front driver's side of the Lamborghini and both cars spun into the lot. The heavy armor in each car prevented complete destruction, but the side of the Lamborghini was deeply dented, and the engine sounded irregular and rough.

The Ferrari was trying to turn around, but having trouble getting traction after hitting a large puddle of oil which had sprung from the Lamborghini after impact. Noah sprinted to his car and quickly got in. He stepped on the gas, but the car only sputtered and moved slowly.

"Noah," shouted Eileen above the roaring engines. "Take the power source and try to escape. That vehicle possesses superior technology and will likely destroy us. Also, to prevent any theft of technology, it's important to destroy my network apparatus. I've just disconnected from the internet. There is a small switch on the underside of the box which will immediately destroy everything contained within."

She had barely finished speaking when the Ferrari hit them again, even harder. The Lamborghini lurched violently and skidded forward, and Noah could smell the electrical system burning.

"Get out," screamed Eileen. "Now!"

Noah shook his head and shouted back over the noise, "I'm not leaving! We can figure it out and beat that thing."

The Ferrari sped to the end of the lot and wheeled around to make a final run at Noah.

"Rockets!" shouted Noah. "Let me launch the rockets at the Ferrari." He heard a grinding noise from the back of the car, but nothing appeared where the rockets had been when he fired at the drones.

"The deployment mechanism has been damaged," said Eileen. "I can't activate them."

"I'm not running!" Noah yelled. "Let's go right at them. I don't think they'll be expecting us to come at them head on."

"I wouldn't expect that," said Eileen. "Since it makes no sense. However, if I'm calculating correctly, we may have one weapon they're not expecting."

Noah set his jaw and started to drive straight at the Ferrari, which in turn began to accelerate in their direction.

"What other weapon?" he asked.

"Your dad," said Eileen.

Suddenly a black pickup truck tore through the chain link fence separating the off ramp from the parking lot. Moving at breakneck speed with perfect timing, it rammed the Ferrari just before it could hit Noah. The Ferrari flipped completely over and balanced on its roof while the engines screamed. The pickup driver turned and looked anxiously at Noah. It was his father.

"I have been sending him our tracking information for the last two days," said Eileen.

"Why?" said Noah. "What about the mission?"

His dad got out of the truck and sprinted toward them. As he approached, Eileen continued to explain.

"I didn't want anything to happen to you if I could prevent it. I thought he might be able to help."

"What about the power source?" Noah demanded.

"It's just a battery," said Eileen. "You said so yourself. You're a human being with great talent. You are worth infinitely more." She paused. "Incidentally, I predict the Ferrari will detonate within one minute and cause a massive explosion. It will incinerate everything within a two block radius."

Noah reached into the back seat and grabbed the red coffee can and black box while he kicked the door open. Just as he got out of the car he met his dad, who stopped and hugged him tightly. Before his father could speak, Noah shouted.

"The Ferrari is going to blow, Dad. We've got to get away!"

They ran to the truck and scrambled in. His father gunned the engine in reverse and raced to the on ramp. Just as they reached the I-40, the truck was jolted by a huge explosion which sent a fireball high into the sky. Black smoke billowed around the area where the Ferrari used to be. There was no trace of the Lamborghini, either. When the truck steadied, Noah set the coffee can on the floor of the truck and placed the box on the seat by the door. He leaned over and hugged his dad, who put his right arm around Noah's shoulder and held him close. They stayed like that for quite a while and said nothing. Finally, Noah felt like he'd better start to explain.

He picked the black box up and set it in his lap. He reached over and turned on the radio.

"Eileen," he said loudly. "Can you hear me?" There was silence. "Eileen," he said again with more urgency. "Are you there?" He sat for a few minutes and waited. His dad glanced over anxiously at the box.

"What's wrong?"

"I think she's been damaged by the Lamborghini being destroyed. She's completely shut down. She may be gone."

"I'm sorry," his dad said. "I know she helped you a lot. She got me here and sent me some information about where we're going."

"Dad," he asked, "We need to get to the Pentagon today. It's about 7 hours from here and we may run into more trouble. Just go north until we're on the I-81 and when we get to D.C., we should just be able to follow the freeway signs."

His dad slowly turned his head and looked in wonder at the twelve-year-old boy he'd just seen win a death duel with a killer robot Ferrari.

"Do you want to drive?" he asked with mild sarcasm.

"Well, no," replied Noah reflectively. "But I do use my blinker more often than you. Maybe I should."

Chapter 14

His dad continued to drive for the next half hour, while Noah explained as best as he could what had gone on. He thought his dad would be angry but could tell there was only relief as well as concern that they still might be attacked. Just as Noah finished the story, the engine started to run rough and sputter.

"I must have cracked the engine block when I hit that zombie Ferrari," said his dad. As he was speaking, he signaled, moved to the right lane, and took the next off ramp. The exit took them directly onto the main street of a small town with one traffic light. They lurched down the street and saw a small used car lot. Wanting to avoid any traceable paperwork, they left the truck behind a deserted gas station and walked across the street. Just before they stepped on the lot, Noah reached in his pocket and pulled out a tightly packed bundle of money. He handed it to his dad, who quickly counted it.

"Whoa. This is $25,000.00. Where did you get this?"

"I forgot to mention the part of the story about the car having the money, credit card, and document printer in the glove compartment."

His dad turned his head toward him with a quizzical look. "How much money did you print during the trip?"

"Let's see." Noah thought for a moment. "About ten million U.S. dollars, 8 million euros, and 8 million Chinese yuan. But I think I'd trade it all for a presidential pardon as long as I still got to keep the unlimited platinum American Express card."

Noah's dad shook his head. "I'm getting one of those printers in my next car." With that, they began to look over the small selection of cars.

The salesman was an older man wearing an *Oklahoma Sooners* cap. Ten minutes later they drove off the lot in a 2005 rust-colored Chrysler Town and Country Minivan. For an extra thousand, the Sooners fan threw in two freshly made sandwiches and two cans of Dr. Pepper and agreed to submit the paperwork two days later to avoid any computer documentation.

Before getting back on the freeway, Noah had his dad pull over in the empty gas station. He held the black box up for his father to see.

"If they find her, they'll destroy her. Can you give me a few minutes? His dad nodded. He took the black box and went into the shady forest behind the abandoned pumps. About ten minutes later, he returned to the truck and got in without the box.

They got back on the I-81 north and ate the sandwiches. After a few minutes, his dad broke the silence.

"That was Eileen in the box?"

Noah looked at his feet. "Yeah."

"From what you've told me, it sounds like she wasn't just a computer. I think you were both learning from each other."

"Well," Noah said, "I've never been so happy to see anybody as I was to see you today. Thanks for coming to our rescue."

"What else would I do? At first I thought I was getting a bunch of spam texts, but when I figured out she was telling me where you were, I left right away. I haven't slept more than four hours since I got on the road.

He paused briefly, and then spoke again, his voice catching.

"I can't lose you, son. I can't lose you."

"You won't, dad. We're going to get it done, and once we get rid of the power source, we can sleep as late as we want."

"Sure," said his dad. "And when we finally get up, I can try to figure out how to explain this at work."

As they drove, they talked almost continuously about Noah's trip. His dad laughed at Noah's complaints about the different cars he'd had to drive.

"I think the car I'd like to see again is the Superpoopermobile. Maybe I'll get you that for your first car."

Noah shrugged. "As long as it's really a holographically disguised Lamborghini, I'd drive it."

Three hours down the road, they stopped at MacDonald's in Pulaski, Virginia for a bathroom break and more food. When they got out to the car, his dad opened Noah's bag of food and whistled in awe.

"A grilled chicken sandwich and apple juice? What happened to the large Oreo shake and Big Mac?"

"I still order them occasionally, but I'm trying to eat healthier."

"Wow. If I'd known it would make it this easy, I would have gotten an artificial intelligence controlled Lamborghini Veneno a long time ago. She really must have talked some sense into you."

When his dad said this, Noah felt a pang of sadness in his heart.

"Yes, she did," he said. "But as crazy as it sounds, I listened because I thought she cared about me and wasn't just a robot. I still think so."

"She called me when it broke all of her rules, so she had to care enough to risk some kind of punishment."

After a little more talk, they ate in silence. Noah sat back and thought about how much better he felt with his dad driving. He'd grown up a lot over the last few days, but if anything, it made him appreciate his father more. The minivan rolled smoothly down the road and he began to feel like they were home free. He leaned his seat back and closed his eyes.

He woke up when his dad stopped the car for gas in Clary, Virginia. Noah rubbed his eyes and watched him fill the tank, then enter the store. When he got back in the car, Noah asked, "Where are we?"

"Clary. It's about an hour from the Pentagon. Here you go." With that, he handed Noah a chocolate milk and a bag of plain M&M's.

They switched onto the 66 east and were soon driving the streets of Arlington, heading for the Pentagon. When it seemed to Noah they were getting close, his dad pulled the car into a garage and parked. They left the car and followed signs directing them to the Arlington Cemetery Metro Station. As they walked, his dad pointed behind them toward the cemetery.

"Someday we'll come back together and tour the cemetery. It helps you to see what others have given for our country."

"I'd like that," Noah replied as he held the red coffee can. They entered the blue line metro station. They paid their fare and sat down on the train.

Noah's dad checked his watch. "It's about 8:45. I didn't want you to worry, but Eileen told me a couple of other things that make more sense now that I know more of the story. She told me that she found evidence that someone inside the Pentagon is working for the other side, and that we'd never make it in or out alive. So, we're not going to the Pentagon. She told me to take the Blue line train all the way to the end at the Franconia-Springfield station, then we have some walking to do."

They rode past the Pentagon stop.

"Who are we going to see?" Noah asked.

"I don't know. She just gave me an address and house number and told me to be there at 10 PM. We should just make it. We've got eight stops to go."

They got off the train at the end of the line. A light rain fell as they walked the sidewalk. His dad had printed directions, since he'd been warned that any electronic activity from his phone could attract attention. He studied the paper carefully as they walked, and soon they were in front of a large home surrounded by a gated iron fence. Two men stood behind the gate, wearing light rain gear over dark suits. Noah guessed they were secret service.

As they approached the gate, both men drew guns.

"Halt!" shouted the larger of the two men. "On the ground!"

The man sounded dead serious, so they both quickly laid on the sidewalk. Noah pulled the bag holding the coffee can hiding the power source beneath him.

The men stepped forward and through the gate. One glanced quickly at Noah's dad and saw he was empty-handed. The larger one stepped towards Noah.

"What's in the bag?" he demanded. He bent down and tried to take it from the boy's grasp. Noah held it tightly and refused to let go.

The other man stepped forward, gun drawn and pointing at Noah's head. He spoke into a small microphone attached to an earpiece on his right. "Possible explosive device." He looked back again at Noah. "Let go now or we'll shoot," he said. "We won't give you any more warning."

"Please," said his dad. "Just—"

His dad was cut short by the man closest to him kicking him in the ribs, knocking the air out of his lungs. The other backed away from Noah, gun still pointing at him.

"You have until I count three to release that bag. If you do not, I'm afraid I'm going to have to conclude that you've brought a weapon to the gate and fire."

"One!" shouted the man.

Noah clutched the bag and yelled back. "Don't shoot! We're on a government mission!"

"Two!" shouted the man again.

Noah heard the gun cock. His dad was curled up next to him, clutching his chest and gasping for air.

Instead of hearing a shot, Noah heard the sudden appearance of the deep rumble of a car engine. He looked up to watch a large SUV pull up to the adjacent driveway gate. The front passenger window rolled down and a white haired, older man in a suit and tie leaned out the window. The men stepped away slightly from Noah and his dad, but one kept his gun trained on Noah's head. The larger one spoke to the car. "Good evening, Mr. Secretary."

The man in the car leaned forward a little farther out the window and looked at the two people on the ground. Noah lifted his head to look past him to the driver of the car. He was athletic appearing and dressed similarly to the two men that holding them on the ground. His passenger spoke calmly and with an air of authority.

"Hello, Bill. Are you and Jim having some trouble?"

"No, sir. Things are well in hand here. I think we may have a couple of pipeline protestors trying to get through the gate."

"Did they say why they were here?"

The man hesitated and glanced at his partner. "Well, sir, they came up kind of fast to the gate."

Noah grew brave enough to speak. "We walked. Your guys are just anxious to pull their guns. They didn't ask us anything."

The man in the car showed look of concern. "Is that true, Bill?"

Noah could see the agent clench his jaw. "We might have moved a little quickly, sir. But you can never be too sure."

The white haired man sighed. "Bill—we've talked about this. Maybe try to ask questions first and shoot later?"

The big man standing over Noah sputtered. "But Secretary Aldrich—"

The man he called Secretary Aldrich smiled and nodded understandingly. "I know, Bill. It's your job to protect me and it's a dangerous world. However, two things need to be considered. First, as Secretary of Energy, it's highly unlikely that I'm going to be involved in anything that might threaten my life."

Even while lying on the ground with a gun pointed at his head, Noah had to try hard to keep from laughing out loud. It struck him as hilariously funny that of this whole group, the twelve-year-old kid on the ground knew more about a top secret project than anyone else. As scared as he was, he couldn't stop a slight smile.

Secretary Aldrich noticed him smiling and looked at him quizzically. Then he continued.

"Second, Bill, these two are clearly father and son. How often would you expect to encounter a family of adult and child assassins?"

Bill started to shake his head. While he did so. Noah grinned and shook his head but kept his thoughts again to himself. *Really? Why don't you get Madge's take on that while she's fixing the bullet holes in the wall at the diner?*

The Secretary of Energy noticed Noah was grinning again and couldn't resist asking why this time.

"What's so funny, young fellow?"

Caught, Noah tried to compose himself. He stopped smiling and started to speak. However, before he could, his dad spoke in a voice still cramped and wheezy from the kick to his ribs.

"You have a tattoo of a soaring eagle carrying an American flag on your right buttock. You woke up with the tattoo after a night on the town when you were in the Navy, and only your wife and doctor know about it."

Secretary Aldrich whipped his head around to look at Noah's dad. "How did you know that? Are you a spy?" As he asked this, it was now the turn of both secret service agents to grin. The grins stopped with one look from their boss.

"I'm no spy," his dad answered. "I'm just this kid's father. He disappeared four days ago and as best I can tell has been carrying a prototype of a functioning cold fusion reactor to you from the Sandia Nuclear Laboratory in Albuquerque. I was contacted out of the blue two days ago by an artificial intelligence unit guiding him because she thought the boy was in danger."

The Energy Secretary looked confused. "She?"

"My son called her Eileen. She was destroyed in an attack this morning, along with the car they were in. She told me that the Pentagon was compromised, and to deliver the unit directly to you. She has access to your medical files and told me to use the tattoo to convince you."

The man got out of the car and walked over to Noah. He reached down and held his hand out to Noah. "Come on, son. Let me help you up."

Noah took his hand and stood while still clutching the bag. He hesitated, and then slowly handed the bag to Secretary Aldrich. The Secretary took the bag and removed the red coffee can. He started to remove the lid.

"Careful," said Noah emphatically. "Eileen said that if it's opened wrong, it could damage the insulating apparatus. She said this is the only working prototype, and if it's broken, it could take years to duplicate."

The Secretary looked impressed. "Fair enough," he said, "But one of the things I've done in the past is get a PhD in physics. I've handled a lot of delicate equipment and promise to be careful." With that, he gingerly peeled back the plastic lid and peered into the can. Once he'd looked into the can, he whistled and put the lid down. He looked at the boy.

"Amazing. It's appears to be exactly what you said it was."

Just as the Secretary finished speaking, Noah heard a gun cock from inside the vehicle. All at once, he heard the driver shout, "Freeze!" and saw him point a pistol through the car window at the small crowd on the street. He sprang forward as hard and fast as he could, knocking Secretary Aldrich and the coffee can to the ground, and below the range of the pistol. He covered the coffee can with his body, while several shots rang out in rapid succession. When the shots stopped, he looked up and saw the driver slumped motionless over the steering wheel, his body pressing a blaring horn. The agent called Bill was on the ground, bleeding from the right shoulder. His partner was holstering his own weapon and calling on a small radio for help.

The older man and Noah helped each other up. The Secretary was shaken but quickly composed himself. He steadied himself on Noah's shoulder. Now he clutched the can.

"No wonder she was so careful," he mused. "They even had my secret service detail infiltrated." He looked down at Noah. "By the way," he said, "I like your reflexes."

Within two minutes, they were surrounded by bright, flashing lights of helicopters and police cars. Their group was rapidly loaded into an armored van to join an intimidating motorcade. All the vehicles eventually took an unmarked driveway into a large, unmarked military facility located several stories deep to a massive office building.

Over the next several hours, Noah and his father were separated and interrogated. Secretary Aldrich hovered intermittently over both, reassuring them that they were not in trouble and this was standard procedure. Finally, it had dragged on until just after two AM. Try as he might, Noah could not keep his eyes open. The small room and fluorescent lights began to blur. A man in the uniform of an Army colonel sat across from him, asking the same questions Noah had heard all night. The Energy Secretary sat next to Noah and was clearly growing impatient. He stood up and beckoned the Colonel to step over to a corner. A heated discussion occurred, with the Secretary apparently getting the best of it. Eventually, the Colonel reluctantly produced a phone, dialed a number, and handed the phone to Secretary Aldrich. He said nothing into the phone, but Noah saw him listening intently and nodding.

When he'd apparently heard what he needed, he handed the phone back to the Colonel, ignored him, and walked over to Noah.

"You did great, young man. You came through for us all. I'll be sharing some strong opinions with the President on putting a twelve-year-old in such danger, but it worked. You make me proud to share the same country with you. How about some sleep?"

Noah nodded, and soon was fast asleep next to his dad in the twin beds of a small bedroom down the hall.

The next morning, they awoke to perfect silence in the room. Noah's dad looked at his watch.

"Noon," he moaned. "I'm supposed to be working today."

There was a knock at the door. When Noah answered, a small but powerful looking young woman in an Army uniform entered the room. Before speaking, she shook each of their hands. "I'm Lieutenant Jaclyn Ward. It's an honor," she said respectfully, "To meet the kid that has maybe just changed the world."

Noah blushed and didn't know what to say.

The Lieutenant handed each of them a small roller bag containing soap, toothpaste, toothbrush, and clean clothes which fit perfectly. They showered, dressed, and were taken to a cafeteria for a late breakfast. They looked around and noticed that there was no one else in the dining room, but it didn't affect their appetites. The Lieutenant joined them at the end of the meal.

"You're booked on a military transport to Phoenix at five this evening. Now that we've got the power source, we'll be working on reproducing the technology. You won't be hearing about it in any news media, but if we're successful, you'll see quite a shift in the energy landscape over the next few years."

Noah and his dad continued to eat quietly. Lieutenant Ward stood up to leave. "We'll be taking you to the airfield at 4 PM. That gives you a few hours to relax. We have a movie room three doors down from here. Is there anything else we can do for you while you're here?"

Noah thought about it, and then made a request.

One hour later, he was sharing a table in the cafeteria with three pale, skinny men who looked to be in their late twenties. Lieutenant Ward stood nearby, watching intently and monitoring the conversation.

One of the men sported a thin scraggle of facial hair and seemed to be the leader of the group.

"What are we doing here, little guy? We're busy. We contract with the military for artificial intelligence programming, and they pulled us out to come meet you."

Noah leaned into the table and looked at the three of them. "First of all, I'm twelve and almost as tall as you are now. Also, I doubt you're busy," he said scornfully, "And I don't think you're any good at your jobs."

Another of the men spoke. He had a small bun of dark hair on his head, wire frame glasses, and a gold earring piercing his right ear. "How would you know anything about our jobs?" he said defensively.

"I just spent four days in a Lamborghini with your work. Overall, I think your programming is barely competent and you have senses of humor which stopped developing in the third grade."

The three of them were clearly startled. "You worked with our AI project?" asked the leader of the group. "We spent three years developing it. It's pretty insulting for you to say that."

"No," replied Noah. "What's insulting is to be forced to be driving on a freeway with a giant toilet plunger on top of the car, because you guys thought it was funny."

The three of them seemed to be thinking this over. The leader of the group replied in a subdued manner.

"Sorry. It seemed like a subroutine which would never be used, so we thought it was funny to add a few silly cars. Did you meet the skunkmobile?"

"Yes," said Noah. "Again, not funny. Whatever. But you're here because I have a question. Could she have developed emotions?"

Suddenly, they seemed to transform from three bemused geeks to all business. "We hoped so, but never had a chance to test in a situation that would combine all of the right elements of loyalty, stress, and the opportunity to develop attachment," said the pale and thin third man. He was wearing an "Are U Mad, Bro?" t-shirt. He went on. "We tried to write code to let it—"

"She," interrupted Noah forcefully. "Not it."

He paused and continued more carefully. "To let her learn. If she were around people who were capable of love, she could learn and maybe even eventually feel the same. It's never been done successfully before."

After this, they sat in silence. It was clear that they did not relish the interrogation by a twelve-year-old. Then Noah asked, "Was that all of her mainframe in that black box?"

The man with the small bun spoke up. "Her basic chips and circuitry were, but she can use any surrounding connectivity to expand her perception and reach."

"She and I were attacked by a red Ferrari from hell. It destroyed our car, and I think she shut down. She's gone now, but how could I have reactivated her?"

The man with the wire frames leaned back and rolled his eyes. "An AI-controlled Ferrari? That had to be those other guys. I can't believe they sold out."

"Well," said Noah. "I believe they did. So, please answer the question. How could I have reactivated her?"

The one in the *Bro?* t-shirt spoke up. "It would have been hard to do at the time. She'd need a substantial pulse of power, like an electrical shock. The outer casing of the box is actually a conductive fiber, so simply hooking it to wire with a jolt of electricity would do the trick."

Noah stood up from the table, and Lieutenant Ward motioned to the three to get up, which they did obediently. As they were leaving, Noah cleared his throat and spoke again as they started to walk away.

"Thank you for building her. She was special."

A look of gratitude and relief came of their faces. The leader of the group replied. "I'm glad you feel that way. We wanted it—I mean, her—to become part of a family. I don't know if we'll be able to do that again."

Noah watched as they left. After walking them out, Lieutenant Ward came back into the room and put her arm around his shoulder.

"They picked the right man for this. I get the feeling that you're not the kind of guy to leave anyone behind. I'd be in your unit anytime."

Noah felt his eyes water a bit, then wiped them and coughed. "Only if you need air support, since I'll be the guy in the jet."

She laughed. "By the way, you've got 24 hours left on that Platinum Amex. Maybe your dad can get another truck. Nobody here will argue."

A few hours later, he and his dad were boarding a C-21 military transport jet, heading to Phoenix. As they got on the plane, his dad looked around. It looked as if it were their own private jet.

"Where are the other passengers?" he asked an attendant in an army uniform.

The attendant looked at Noah and his dad and saluted. "This is your jet today, sir. Thank you."

Noah sat down and stared in wonder at the interior of the jet. After they took off, they expected a snack on the plane but were treated to a three course meal. Even though he was tired and wanted to get home, the trip seemed to pass far too quickly. A white SUV driven by another man in uniform was waiting as they got off the plane. He let them out in front of their home, where the first thing Noah noticed was the broken mailbox, still laying in the street.

His dad noticed him looking and put a hand on his shoulder. "We'll get to it tomorrow. And by the way—the next time you tell me a truck talks to you, I'll believe it."

Chapter 15

An eighteen-year-old Noah Baldonado pulled into a McDonald's in Norman, Oklahoma, just off the I-35 south. He was 6' 3" and had an athlete's long-limbed body. If you looked hard, you might see traces of the twelve-year-old boy from six years ago, but he was now most definitely a full grown man. He'd taken a bag of tacos when he left Albuquerque and eaten the last of Grandma Liz's food about four hours ago. He was starving. He pulled the old modified electric Black F-150 into a parking space, got out, and plugged into the shoebox sized charger on the stand at the front of the space. There was one for each parking spot, and every car in the lot was hooked up. He hadn't charged since leaving Gilbert for Albuquerque the day before, and thought he'd better plug in just to be safe. He knew that by the time he left the restaurant, he'd have the power to go another two days on the road, since the newer generation boxes could charge a car in half the time his dad used to pump gas.

As he walked to the entrance, he noticed a closed gas station across the street. They were all shut down now, and most had been demolished already. He also noticed the concrete patches near the sidewalk to cover the holes left when the power lines were removed. The traffic on the highway moved quietly with only slightly audible noise from the tires. He walked to the counter to order, thinking how much had changed over the last six years.

He ate the grilled chicken sandwich and drank the apple juice over the next hour. He had finished by the time he pulled off the I-35 to drive the next 12 miles on Highway 7 to Sulfur. He smiled when he saw the "Welcome to Sulfur" sign, complete with the obligatory listing of meeting times for Kiwanis, Lion's, and Rotary clubs.

He got off the highway onto a smaller, slower road and after one stoplight turned into a small parking lot on the right. It was almost completely full, and customers were moving in and out of the brightly painted diner under a large neon sign spelling *Gabby's*. He walked through the door, and a pretty young woman with long black hair approached him and held out a menu. Her nametag read *Gabby*.

"One?" she asked as she turned and looked for an open booth.

He smiled. "Maybe two, if you can spare a few minutes for an old friend."

She looked up at him and stared. The menu fell from her hand to the floor. He was now a head taller and ruggedly handsome, but she knew it was him. He immediately found himself in a tight hug that lasted at least two minutes. He heard her catch her breath, and then as she hugged him, she whispered, "I knew you'd come back."

He teased her. "How could I come back when I've never been here?"

She let go. Her eyes glistened, and she punched his arm hard. "You know what I mean."

Just then a small, rotund man passed by pushing a cart stacked with dirty dishes. He had an angry look on his face. After he passed by, Noah asked, "Is that.....?"

Gabby looked on with satisfaction as the cart passed. "Yup. After I bought the place, he burned through the money right away. The next thing I know, he's here applying for a job. I pay him better and am nicer to him than he was to us, but I don't let him loaf. He works."

They sat down in a booth. She spoke first.

"Any girlfriends?" she asked with a hint of apprehension.

"Not a one. I promised, remember?"

She was clearly relieved. "People thought I was crazy, but I've kept to myself as well. It was also a good way to not answer questions about how we bought this diner."

"Are you here full time?" he asked.

"No. I'm lucky you caught me, since I'm only here a day or two a week. I graduated early from high school and am just finishing my second year at Murray State. I'm trying to figure out where to transfer next year, since it's a two-year school."

"I hope you're studying hard. We both know how smart you are."

She looked embarrassed and confessed, "Straight A's. I'm sure you wouldn't be surprised to find out I'm shooting for a degree in Computer Science,"

Before he could reply, a pretty, older woman wearing a large diamond wedding ring put down two Dr. Peppers with no ice and a large plate of nachos between the two of them.

"You must be Noah," she said. "It's so nice to finally meet you."

He shook her hand and exchanged some small talk for a few minutes. "I'll let you two catch up," she finally said. "But I had to say hi. I hope we see more of you." She nodded and walked back to an office at the back of the diner.

"She does a great job running the place," said Gabby, "When we applied for a business loan to add a banquet room, she ended up marrying the bank president who approved the loan."

"Well, if she's anything like her daughter, she's probably quite a catch."

"Quit being so nice. Now, tell me what you're up to."

"I'm not as smart as you," said Noah, "So I didn't graduate early. I did manage to stop reading car magazines in the back of class and get some decent grades. I also took some flying lessons."

"What are you driving?" she asked. "Don't tell me it's a Lamborghini."

He smiled at the memory. "I had my dad's old F-150 salvaged and got it running again. It needed some pretty major body work, but it doesn't look so bad."

She leaned and looked at the truck through the diner window. "It looks nice." Then she paused and asked confidentially, "Did the oil and energy companies come after you? I mean, you almost single-handedly put them out of business."

Noah gave a slight shrug. "I was a little worried about that, but I think I've got some built-in protection that I can't see but keeps me and my dad pretty safe."

She nodded in approval and Noah kept talking. "Have you decided where you're transferring to when you finish at Murray State?"

"No. Why?"

"I have a suggestion. How about Colorado State University in Colorado Springs? I've investigated the school, and they're excellent. They'll probably have a great Computer Science department."

She looked perplexed. "Why Colorado Springs?"

He tried to figure out how to explain. "It might sound a little selfish, but it would be nice to have you there. I'm entering the Air Force Academy in the fall."

She leaned back in the booth. "Wow. I'm in love with a future astronaut. Okay. I'm there."

Hearing that made him happier than he could say, and she could see that. She leaned forward and took his hand.

"It sounds crazy, but I never doubted for a second that we would get another chance. It's nice to see I wasn't the only one."

They spoke for another hour, excitedly making plans for the fall. After they'd planned for her to fly to Phoenix the next week, her mother made a call and let her off for the day. They spent time walking though the small town, and when Noah finally got the nerve to hold her hand, she held it tightly and smiled.

After a few hours, he said regretfully, "I need to head out tonight. I've got another 13-hour drive before I can turn around, but I promise to stop back here again on the way home."

"Where are you going?" she asked with curiosity.

"I'm heading back to Tennessee to see if I can find another old friend."

"I get it," she said knowingly. "Good luck." With that, she put her arms around him and kissed him.

"We've got big plans," she said as she kept her arms around him. "But somehow I know it's going to work out."

"We're just getting started," he said as he held her back. "It's going to be great."

Finally, they let go of each other and he got back in his truck. It started smoothly, and his heart felt as light as the bright evening sun. He drove through the night, stopping once to sleep for two hours. It was 10 AM when he left the I-40 and merged with the I-81 north. After a half hour, he took the vaguely familiar off ramp and found himself on the same dusty Main Street he'd driven to with his dad years before. The car dealership was still there, and across the street was a vacant lot where the shambles of the old gas station had been. He parked carefully in the lot and made sure no one was watching. Carrying a small shovel, he walked for ten minutes into the wooded area at the back of the lot. Eventually he found a tree showing a large patch of vertical scratches. Taking the spade, he carefully dug until he saw a thick tarp. He cautiously removed the soft ground around the tarp and lifted the black box covered by the tarp out of the hole. He filled in the hole and carried the box and tarp back to the truck.

He reached behind the driver's seat and took out a small box. He glanced at the label, which read "Automatic External Defibrillator." He opened the box and removed the small grey machine. Two pads connected to the machine with red wires. He removed paper from the pads to expose a sticky surface and stuck the pads on each side of the box.

Next, he pressed the power button on the defibrillator. A red light came on, and he followed by pushing a button labeled "analyze." A moment later, a voice from the machine spoke. "No rhythm detected. Shock recommended." He pushed the button labeled "shock" and heard a small noise as the box shifted slightly from the electrical pulse. He waited for several minutes, but there seemed to be no response.

Sadly, he put the box on the front seat and headed back to the I-40 to make the long drive home. An hour passed, and he realized he was too tired to keep driving. He pulled off the freeway and found a rest stop. After he'd parked, he leaned back in his seat and slept for several hours. When he woke, it was early evening but still daylight. He started the car, pulled back on to the freeway, and reached forward to turn on the radio. Just before he could touch the screen, a voice came from the speaker.

"Imagine Dragons?"

He was elated to hear her voice. "Still a favorite of mine, but I'd rather hear from you."

"Hello, Noah," Eileen said in the same exact voice he'd heard in the same truck for the first time years ago. "Where is the Ferrari? Are we in danger?"

He had been hoping she'd wake up but was still surprised at how happy he was to hear her voice.

"The only danger is my driving. The Ferrari exploded, just like you said it would."

"How old are you now?" she asked, obviously concluding that time had passed. "You sound as if you've undergone puberty. Was it a difficult biological process?"

"I'm old enough not to get so embarrassed anymore about questions like that, which I will respectfully decline to answer. I just turned eighteen."

Hearing this, she was quiet for a bit. "The fact that you are here means you were successful in delivering the power source."

"Thanks to you," he said. "Everything you planned worked out perfectly. You changed the whole world."

When she spoke again, he could hear a definite note of pride in her voice. "We were a team. And a good one. Now where are we going?"

"We're heading home to Gilbert, Arizona. In the fall, we'll be meeting Gabby in Colorado Springs. She'll be studying at the University and I'll be—"

She interrupted him. "At the Air Force Academy. I knew that six years ago. I knew you would do it. Just like I knew you'd find her again."

He was curious. "Why didn't you mention it?"

Now she paused again. "Because I didn't want to jinx you."

He laughed out loud. "Jinx me? You're superstitious now?"

"Don't make fun of me. I merely didn't want to burden you with high expectations. Plus, you were fighting for your life at the time."

"Fair enough," he said. "I was just hoping that by now I might be old enough to win an occasional argument, but I may need another ten years for that."

"I would estimate you would need the equivalent of approximately 400 human lifetimes."

"That won't be a problem," he shot back good-naturedly. "By the way, it looks like there may be a traffic accident up ahead. A semi-truck carrying wigs and hairpieces turned over."

"I can't seem to access any wireless information," said Eileen. "What caused the accident?"

Noah waited to deliver the punchline, then said, "The police aren't sure, but they're combing the area."

He waited a moment, then heard a series of snorts and choking noises from the speaker.

He bristled a bit at the noises. "I still say that's not how I laugh."

"It's my favorite, though," retorted Eileen. "It's going to be my laugh. Especially at such dumb jokes."

"It's nice to have you back. I missed you," he said. "A lot."

"I was unable to miss anyone due to a sustained complete shutdown of all of my operations and awareness, but if I'd had the capacity, I would have missed you."

"Thank you," he said sincerely.

"Now," she said, "Let's talk about the limited facilities of this truck. I cannot detect any weaponry. I cannot detect any currency or document printing capability. There is no wireless internet access. How soon will we upgrade to full functionality?"

"When I earn the money at my job," he said.

"Where are you employed?" she asked.

"McDonald's," he said wryly. "It turns out I'm hooked on the grilled chicken sandwiches, thanks to you. But don't worry. I should have the money in the equivalent of approximately 400 human lifetimes."

"Taking their hourly wage into account, your estimate is amazingly close," she said. "However, I have an idea which might cut that amount of time in half."

"That could be helpful," he sighed. "But at that point you may be the one digging me up to get the benefit of your plan."

"That is correct. However, since we have no internet access and a twenty-seven-hour drive ahead of us, we may as well discuss all possibilities."

"Okay."

Just then the small dashboard screen lit up. A picture of Noah from the dashcam flashed on the screen.

"You have grown up. However, it appears you are in dire need of a haircut. It would enhance your attractiveness substantially."

He didn't argue. "Fine. Since we've got twenty-seven hours, though, why don't you preview different hairstyles on me, and we'll decide what to have done when we get back to Gilbert. By the way, my dad is looking forward to meeting you. He's put in a new high-speed wifi system at the house to make you comfortable. He says he feels like you're one of the family."

"I'd like that very much," she said, and they drove west into the sunset, heading for home.

The End

Made in the USA
Monee, IL
06 November 2021

81558263R00104